"Do you know what's going to happen between us?"

"I know the basics." *Didn't she sound all worldly and wise.*

He hooked his finger between two buttons of her uniform at the gap that sometimes showed between her breasts. "We're going to have to sleep together."

He moved her backward until she felt the edge of the counter pushing against her hips. "Just wanted you to know."

"You'll do it?" A thousand different emotions pushed through her until her breath seemed to stall inside her, and she grew light-headed.

"Yeah," he replied, "I'll do it."

The way he emphasized the word *it* made her toes curl. Nell let out a long breath. The last thing on her list would be completed. "Well, thank you, Riley." She stepped sideways and turned to leave. Not that *leave* was the right word—*escape* was closer to the truth.

Riley grabbed her arm and spun her to face him. "We haven't hashed out the details yet."

Books by J. M. Jeffries

Kimani Romance

Virgin Seductress

J. M. JEFFRIES

is the collaboration between two women who are lifelong romance-aholics. Jacqueline Hamilton grew up believing that life should always have a happy ending. Being a military brat, she has lived in some of the most romantic places in the world. As an almost-lawyer, Jackie decided to chuck it all, live her dream and become a writer.

Miriam Pace grew up believing in fairy tales. She found her prince charming and has been married to him for thirty-seven years. Now a granny, she is reading fairy tales to her grandson.

J. M. JEFFRIES
VIRGIN SEDUCTRESS

KIMANI
ROMANCE

KIMANI PRESS™

ISBN-13: 978-0-373-86030-2
ISBN-10: 0-373-86030-7

VIRGIN SEDUCTRESS

www.kimanipress.com

Printed in U.S.A.

Dear Reader,

First of all, thank you for choosing our book. Remember when you were little and you always thought to yourself that one of these days you would go on a grand adventure and live your dream? Didn't you think you'd have to do it in some exotic locale, far away from where you were born and from the people who love you? Isn't it nice to know that sometimes the greatest adventure can be found in your own backyard with the boy next door? We hope you enjoy reading about Nell and Riley and their grand adventure. Here's to your next adventure. May you find happiness and love along the way.

Much love,

Miriam and Jackie

aka J. M. Jeffries

Jackie: For my father, Earl Alexander Hamilton, you taught me the magic of dreams and the power of wishes. I have loved you since my first breath and I will miss you until my last. For Miriam, this would never have been possible if you didn't believe in me. You are the ultimate fairy godmother.

Miriam: To my husband, Parker, thank you for your love, your loyalty and your perpetual faith in me. When I was writing stories and hiding them, you taught me to believe in myself. I would not be at this point in my life and my career without your incredible belief that I would succeed. To Jackie: You have brought so much energy to my life, I can never thank you enough. This book is your gift.

Acknowledgment

For Sherrie, you put up with us and in our book that earns you the Nobel Peace Prize. "Never thought you'd get one of those, huh?"

Prologue

Wayloo, Mississippi

Nell Evans gripped the armrest of the navy leather chair in her grandmother's lawyer's office. "How much money did she leave me?" She doubted it was too much. She and her grandmother had lived simple lives.

Billy Ray Cross swiped the snow-white handkerchief across his balding forehead. "Including stocks, bank accounts, a few outstanding loans and property after estate taxes, Miss Sarah left you about eighteen-point-five."

Numb, she gazed out of the office window and

studied the statue of Robert E. Lee on a rearing horse in the town square. Nell flexed her fingers hoping to get some feeling back. Eighteen point five *what?* Thousand? Hundred thousand? Her mind refused to go beyond that. There was no way her grandmother could have had anything more than that. Was there?

"Nell, honey?"

"Hundred?" Not possible, she thought even as the word left her mouth. Grandmother had complained over every little expenditure and when gas prices had passed the two-dollar mark, she'd parked the old big-as-a-boat Buick away in the garage and insisted Nell walk everywhere.

"Million." Billy Ray grinned over the tops of his steepled fingers. "Give or take."

The least he could do was look as shocked as she felt. "Oh, my," she croaked. She tried to swallow the lump in her throat. Her face got hot. Her heart raced as if it would burst out of her chest. She was too young to have a heart attack, but her chest was tightening. Panic and disbelief set in. Inhaling deeply, she tried to get some air into her lungs before she fainted.

Billy Ray leaned forward and grabbed a glass pitcher of water off his desktop. He turned over a glass and started pouring some water into it. "Nell, honey, are you okay?" He stopped pouring and held out the glass to her. "You want some water?"

Her hand was shaking so badly, she refused, afraid she'd drop the glass. Instead, she licked dry lips and fanned her hot face. Eighteen-point-five million! She almost pinched herself. Not possible. This just wasn't possible. Where had all that money come from? "Are you sure? There has to be some kind of mistake."

"No mistake."

Feeling a bit calmer, Nell tried to think how this could have happened. The diner her grandmother had owned and where Nell worked didn't generate the kind of money that would produce eighteen million dollars. This had to be a mistake. Only a few days before she'd died, her grandmother had scolded Nell for leaving the light on in the bathroom. *Money doesn't grow on trees.* She had taught Nell how to stretch a dollar, but eighteen-point-five million dollars was almost ridiculous. "But my grandmother was such a…a tightwad. She couldn't—"

"Honey," Billy Ray said as he put the glass on the table then pushed it toward her, "you done hit the mother lode. Be happy."

Well, no kidding. Her grandmother clipped coupons. Used soap until it was a sliver. Wrapped presents in the Sunday comics. The room spun for a second, but Nell took a deep breath and steadied herself. She picked up the glass and gulped the water down. "I don't understand. Where did all this money come from?" *Grandmother,* she silently chided the dead woman, *you kept secrets from me.*

"Miss Sarah was a right smart woman who saved and invested wisely. She just lived like she didn't have a dime." He loosened his tacky hula-girl tie. "Matter of fact, I wouldn't be surprised if she didn't still have her first dime."

Nell opened her mouth to speak. But nothing came out. Her mind couldn't quite grasp the fact that she was an heiress. An heiress! Just like Paris Hilton. She blew out a long breath and forced her hands to stop shaking. Her life had just taken a strange turn for the better.

Eighteen-point-five million dollars! That would buy a lot of dreams. Dreams she'd kept tight inside her for so many years, afraid even to write them down in her journal. With that kind of money she could do anything she wanted, including her most cherished dream of quitting the diner, moving to New York and creating a new life for herself. She could go to college. She could buy a swank New York apartment. She could go to the theater, to galleries, to museums. Walk through Macy's or Sak's Fifth Avenue and buy anything she wanted. Finally she could see Times Square and take a carriage ride through Central Park!

Outside, a little boy on a brand-new bike pedaled down the street, passing Doolittle's Five and Dime. Not that anything was only five or ten cents anymore, but the name had never changed despite the advancement of inflation. Nell thought of all the times she'd shopped the clearance racks at the back of the store, paying as little as she could for the cheapest anything. She could finally purchase air-conditioning. She could…she could…she didn't know what, her mind was frozen. "My grandmother wasn't crazy, was she? I mean, I would have known if she'd lost her mind? Right?"

"Rest easy. Miss Sarah wasn't crazy. She just grew up in the Depression, Nell." Billy Ray shrugged as though he could make her understand a vital element of her grandmother's personality. "It's not uncommon for people from that time to hoard everything they could. At least she didn't stuff the money in her mattress. She put every penny she could into CDs, money markets and stock. Miss Sarah had a pretty shrewd grasp of the stock market and wasn't afraid to take a few risks."

Billy Ray opened a manila folder on top of his desk and picked up a pink envelope. "I think this might help you. She made me promise I'd give it to you after I told you about the money." He held it out to her. "She had me write it out for you. She had the shakes so bad toward the end all she could do was sign."

Nell's hand shook as she took the envelope. Her first instinct was to refuse the letter. Part of her didn't want to know. She could smell a hint of lavender on the heavy paper. Her grandmother had always smelled of lavender. "Should I read it now?"

He nodded. "I know what's in the letter."

He actually blushed. Was the letter embarrassing? What other secrets could her grandmother have? Carefully she slid her finger under the sealed flap.

That way she could use it again, just like her grandmother used to do. The pages crinkled in her cold fingers as she unfolded the letter.

My Dearest Nell,
For so long I've kept you tied to me. I didn't start out that way, but as I grew older, I was afraid of being alone again. I lost my husband. I lost my daughter when she ran off, and I survived both of those hardships. When your mama dropped you off as a baby, you were my second chance to get things right. I held you so tight I didn't let you take a breath without me next to you. I don't think I could have lost you and lived another minute. Please forgive me for manipulating you into keeping an old woman company. You are young and full of dreams, ones I tried to keep you from fulfilling. Forgive me. Know this, I love you with all my heart. I hope this helps you find your place in the world. Go to New York. Go to college. Be the woman you are meant to be.
Grandmother.

Nell's bottom lip began to tremble. Her throat went dry. Her grandmother did love her, but she'd deceived her. How could Nell make up for all this wasted time? She'd put her dreams aside to take care of her grandmother, to keep her company, to be a good girl. A hot tear slipped down her cheek. Who was she supposed to be now?

Nell Evans: Heiress. That didn't fit right. And she wasn't sure it ever would.

Chapter 1

Nine Days Later

Riley Martin heard his black Labrador, Chester, bark. Tucked beneath the undercarriage of his truck, oil dripping down his neck, he turned his head, straining to see what, or who, Chester was barking at.

From between the passenger-side wheels of his truck, he watched a pair of sensible white shoes beneath shapely legs and calves the color of warm clover honey making their way up his driveway. His heart raced.

The only woman in Wayloo who had sexy calves

and sensible shoes was Nell Evans. Sweet un-
touchable Nell. He felt a stirring in his groin and
almost groaned. When had he sunk so low that
waitress shoes could give him a woodie? Damn,
how embarrassing. He had no control over this.
"Down, boy," he murmured. He wasn't some thir-
teen-year-old boy in the throes of hormonal ram-
pages anymore. He was twenty-five years old,
almost twenty-six, and old enough to know better.
But then this was Nell, the source of any number of
wet dreams over the years and awkward silences
when he was with her. Nell did that to him. Unless
he was ordering dinner from her at the diner, or
chitchatting about the weather, he was never quite
sure what to say to her when he really wanted to ask
her to go out with him.

Chester's black-furred legs joined Nell's on the
strip of smooth pavement. "Hi, Nell," Riley called.

After a few seconds of silence, she bent down and
peered beneath the truck. Tendrils of curly blue-
black hair fell forward across her pretty cheeks. "Hi,
Riley."

He smiled. "What can I help you with?" Thoughts
of what he wanted to help her do ran through his
head at lightning speed. Massage oil came to mind.
His palms started to sweat, so he put his wrench
down before he dropped it on his head.

Nell pushed a stray tendril behind her ear. "Do
you have a minute?"

She wanted a minute with him. Only a minute! To

do her properly he'd need five days and fifty cans of whipped cream. Like that would ever happen. But he could dream. "Yeah, give me a second and I'll be right with you."

He worked his way out from beneath his truck and stood. Reaching into his pocket he pulled out an old rag and cleaned off his hands.

Nell had an attractive flush to her light brown cheeks. She chewed her bottom lip. Her hands were stuffed in the pockets of her bubblegum-pink waitress uniform, but he could see her fingers flex inside them. Wisps of curly black hair had worked their way loose from the tight bun at the nape of her neck. Despite the heat, the front of her uniform was buttoned up tight to her throat.

Just once before he died, he wished she'd flash him some of that spectacular cleavage she always kept hidden. Scanning her ripe curves, he had to stop his tongue from falling out of his mouth. She had one hell of a body. All curvy and round and womanly, it was a body crafted for a good time. She was the eighth deadly sin wrapped in pink polyester. And he so wanted to sin.

Hell, he'd dreamed about her luscious body for twelve of his last twenty-five years. And twenty-five years from now, he'd still be dreaming about that body. What he would do for a glimpse. Of course, Nell would have something to say about that.

What was he thinking? Her answer would be a polite but firm no. That was Nell in a nutshell. Buttoned up and hemmed-in didn't come any better than Nell.

He stuffed greasy hands into the pockets of his coveralls and rolled back on his heels. "What can I do for you, Nell?" *Kiss you? Bed you? Lick you all over? Be your sex slave? I'm open for suggestions.*

"Can we go into the house?"

Nell alone with me in the house? This was a straight-up dream come true. *Sweet.* "Sure."

"Thank you."

She walked ahead of him, which gave him a prime opportunity to watch the seductive sway of her heart-shaped butt. Beyoncé, eat your heart out.

"Riley?"

He jerked to a stop and realized they were on the veranda and she seemed to be waiting. "Yeah?"

"The door?" she asked, her eyebrows raised.

Riley tried to bring himself out of his Nell-induced daze. "What?"

Nell faced him, an odd expression on her face. "Are you…are you going to open the door for me?" She raised her eyebrows and clutched her Texas-sized brown vinyl purse to her chest.

Riley wondered how long he'd been so deeply mired into Nell fantasy nine hundred and forty-seven that he'd forgotten where he was. Holding up his dirty hands, he said, "Could you get the door handle? Dirty hands." He didn't want to touch his brand-spanking-new antique brass handle with greasy hands. Of course, not opening a door for a lady would have sent his dead great-grandmother running for her leather strap so she could pop him on the butt for bad manners.

Nell tilted her gaze away, her cheeks going a darker red. "Of course."

He loved making her blush. Somehow she seemed more alive. More touchable. And how he wanted to touch. "I have some sweet tea in the fridge. Would you like a glass?" he asked as they entered the cool interior of the house.

"That would be nice. Thank you." She gave him a shy smile. "Would you like some, too?"

"That would be great." Always so polite and ladylike, she never ceased to amaze him. "Go sit in the kitchen, while I wash up."

"Just take your time. I'm in no hurry." She headed toward the kitchen, her rubber-soled shoes a whisper on the polished wood floor.

The husky lilt of her sultry voice wrapped around him like silk. There wasn't much about her that didn't ring his bells. Riley watched her sway down the long hallway to the kitchen.

When she disappeared into the kitchen, he raced up the stairs two at a time. He ran to the end of the hall and into his bedroom, peeling off his sweaty coveralls and thinking if he was stealthy enough he could con her into an impromptu let-me-jump-your-bones dinner.

He took the fastest shower that he ever had. All the while his mind was racing, wondering if he had enough food in the refrigerator in case he could coax her into staying for said sexy dinner. Visualizing the contents of his refrigerator, he frowned. He had four to-go boxes from the diner, since he ate there almost every night. Not a lot to choose from. Nothing he could throw together and impress her with. He hoped green stuff hadn't grown on them.

Then he remembered he had steaks. New York cuts. Chloe had gone shopping yesterday and brought over a pity basket for him. And they were thawed out. Thank God he was still friends with his ex-wife. He could fire up the grill and he'd be the dinner hero. He could make corn. He always had canned corn because he loved it.

Calm yourself down, boy. You'll be done before you even started proper.

Checking his face in the mirror, he realized he had a bit of stubble on his chin, but decided just to leave it. Shaving would take too much time. Besides a girl he'd dated a few months back had told him it made him look sexy and wild. Sexy and wild was a good thing. Right? God, what was up with him? He was acting like a lovesick puppy dog.

When he was certain he smelled decent and his hair had been tamed, he went to the closet and yanked a black denim shirt off a hanger. He found his last pair of clean jeans slung over his leather reading chair. He had to make some quality time for laundry, especially since his housekeeper Mrs. Clark wouldn't be home from visiting her pregnant daughter for another two weeks.

He ran down the stairs barefooted. About halfway down he stopped. Where the hell were his socks and shoes?

"Riley? Where are you?" Nell's sweet sensual voice saved him from sinking further into thoughts of a past he could never repair.

"Right here." He entered the bright kitchen.

She leaned against the center island's butcher block he'd built, beneath the wrought-iron pot holder with the copper pots and pans he'd never learned how to use since he didn't know to cook. He just liked the way the shiny pots reflected the sun in the morning. "Didn't mean to take so long."

She bent slightly and patted Chester on the head. "That's all right."

For the first time since she'd walked up his driveway, he wondered why she was here. Probably about the trellis on her house damaged by last week's freak storm. He'd promised to get to that soon. "Is it the trellis in the backyard?"

Her eyes widened. "I beg your pardon?"

"The trellis. You remember. Last week. Storm. Trellis." With his hand, he mimicked the trellis falling down in the wind. "I know I promised to fix it, but things have been..." His voice trailed away.

She smiled sweetly. "No, no. I mean, yes it still needs repair, and I know you'll get that done, but I didn't come to discuss the trellis."

He opened the refrigerator and grabbed the glass pitcher full of sweet tea, the only thing besides scrambled eggs he really could make with any degree of confidence.

He used to be much better at seduction.

He smiled at Nell, who looked away, the color on her cheeks deepening. Don't rush her. Let her think it was all her idea. "So why are you here?"

Nell tugged at the tight white collar of her pink uniform. "Did you like being an architect?" she asked instead of answering his question. He could see she was nervous and his curiosity grew stronger. What was on her mind?

Riley prided himself on his ability to put women at ease. He set the pitcher on the tiled counter and took two glasses out of the cabinet. He poured iced tea into each glass. "Yes and no. I liked the creativity, but not all the detail work. I like restoring old homes better." He handed her the glass of tea.

She took a sip. "Did you like living in Chicago?"

He wondered what she was getting at. He watched, fascinated, as her little pink tongue moved slowly over her bottom lip. He caught his breath and gripped the back of the countertop. Have mercy!

"Are you okay?" Nell asked, looking concerned.

Another illicit fantasy flitted through his mind. "Fine. What did you say?"

She sipped her tea and took a moment to set the glass down before looking up at him again. "Did you like living in Chicago?"

He'd hated Chicago and once Chloe had wanted to be close to her aging parents he'd been happy to leave. "Not really. I'm a small-town boy at heart." Forcing himself to let her take the lead was killing him. *Let's just jump on the dining room table and get to the fun stuff.* Though he knew that would never happen no matter how he prayed for it. Nell Evans wasn't the type of girl to jump into any man's bed.

She took a deep breath, showing off her voluptuous breasts at their very best. "I want to ask you if you would do something for me."

Riley raised an eyebrow. Here it comes. He looked deep into the chocolate-brown eyes that had haunted his innermost fantasies for most of his life. He could deny her nothing. "Anything."

"Would you teach me about sex?"

Chapter 2

Okay, Nell thought, at the look of shock on Riley's face. Maybe the direct approach wasn't the wisest choice of action. As Riley continued to remain silent, his hand wrapped around the empty glass, astonishment showed on his face and in his deep brown eyes.

Her confidence began to deteriorate. Somehow, in the cold light of day, the idea she'd had in the deep of the night didn't seem logical anymore. She'd been dreaming about the future and realized she had her future in the palm of her hand. She could finally, after so many years, make her dream a reality. She could finally go to New York, go back to school to become something other than poor, old, boring inexperienced Nell. But how was she going to fulfill her aspirations of being the quintessential New York City sophisticate if she was still a virgin?

Riley blinked at her a couple of times, then shook his head and screwed his finger in his ear. "Would you say that one more time for me?"

Wiping damp palms on her uniform, she swallowed the lemon-sized lump in her throat. She knew Riley wasn't attracted to her. He liked pretty women. Thin women. Women who had perfected the art of conversation.

"I was wondering if…" she said in a timid tone. "Well, if you could…teach me how…" She stared at her shoes, noticing she had a spot of country gravy on the left tip and a smear of what looked like peanut butter on the right one. "About sex?"

He just stood there with his mouth open, staring at her as though he couldn't believe her. She didn't blame him. He had some of the most beautiful women in three states lining up to seduce him. Why would he even entertain the notion of making love to her?

He leaned against the counter, seeming to ponder her words.

Nell had to admit she just liked looking at him. He was tall and well-built, with the grace of a dancer and the movements of a panther. Wide shoulders tapered down to a trim waist and strong muscular thighs. His skin was a lovely shade of light cinnamon and his hair was cut close to his scalp. Little droplets of water still sparkled on the surface of his black hair.

Once upon a time, she'd dreamed about marrying

and starting a family with someone like him. But those young-girl dreams had been abandoned as the years crept by and very few men had showed any romantic interest in her. But the times had changed. Now a horde of single men—and a few not-so-single men— were attempting to insert themselves into her life since word had spread about her inheritance. Greed was a huge incentive for any man to ask out a prissy, plain Jane like herself. "Riley, did you hear what I said?"

He slipped a finger under her chin and forced her head up to meet his gaze. "Why?"

The tip of his finger was warm on her skin. She tried to move away, but her feet refused to move. She even attempted to look away, but his eyes held hers. The intensity of his gaze burned her to the spot. "I have several reasons."

"Name one."

"Well—" She shouldn't have come. Instinct told her to back herself away and hope he forgot she'd ever made this silly suggestion.

She took a deep breath. In for a penny, in for a pound, her grandmother had always said. "Because I'm going to move to New York City." Boy, did that sound dumb, but she simply didn't know what else to say.

He blinked again, and opened his mouth, but no words came out.

Oh, boy, she needed to say something else— something that made sense. "And because you're the only single man in this town who hasn't been calling me up on the phone, sending me flowers, sending me candy or telling me I'm the most beautiful thing that ever graced the planet now that I'm an heiress and have enough money to keep a good man in comfort. Frankly, that makes me think you like me just because I'm me. And that's why you would be perfect." Okay, she'd said it all, the words tumbling out of her mouth in a torrent.

Riley nodded, but didn't say anything for a few seconds as if he needed to give her words time to sink in and make sense. He took his finger from under her chin. "I do like you for you, but what does moving to New York have to do with you needing to learn about sex?"

How did she explain her big dream without sounding dumb? It all made sense in her head. In New York, she didn't have to be boring old Nell Evans, diner waitress and granddaughter of the stingiest woman in Mississippi. Nor did she have to be the daughter of the easiest woman in Mississippi—a woman who didn't even know who of all the men she'd slept with, had been Nell's father. In New York, Nell could be the woman she wanted to be. The one she knew in her heart she was destined to be. She just didn't want to go there with her backwoods country ways showing like a ripped hem on her skirt. "I can't be there and be a virgin."

His dark eyes widened. "You're still a virgin?" His voice held an almost reverent tone.

She could feel a tingly heat infuse her cheeks. "Yes."

"How did that happen?" He ran both his hands over his dark hair. "Or how didn't it happen?"

Sex hadn't happened because Nell wasn't exactly the prettiest or most flirtatious girl in town. Nor was she exactly thin. And it didn't help that her grandmother knew everyone in town and had had the ability to intimidate a marble statue into staying away from Nell. "Well, no one really ever asked me out, that is until I inherited millions of dollars."

"You sound a little bitter."

Yes, she was bitter. She'd spent her whole life in Wayloo and not one man had ever been interested until she became the town's version of a cash cow. Who wouldn't be bitter?

Since gossip about the will had spread, she'd been getting phone calls and had been sent flowers from every man in town who had aspirations toward wealth. Including the men who'd laughed at her in high school.

"You're twenty-five years old, Nell," he continued. "A fully-grown woman."

She rolled her eyes. He hadn't been forced to live in the maximum-security prison her grandmother had called a house, where her every move was accounted for. She had stayed with her grandmother out of guilt and some twisted attempt to win the old woman's love.

Being a good girl had always earned her the only praise her grandmother had thought to issue. "I know how old I am. And trust me, I know about my lack of a social life." She had to get out of his house and find herself a large rock to hide under and hope he'd never ever mention her being here. Or what she'd asked of him. Suddenly, the embarrassment was too much for her.

He crossed his arms over his powerful chest and rocked back on his heels. "I did."

"You did what?"

"Ask you out." He held up three long fingers. "Three times."

How could he have been serious? No one paid her any mind. All the boys in the area had only wanted to date the pretty girls and she'd never measured up. Too shy and self-conscious, she'd always felt everyone was laughing at her behind her back. "You weren't serious."

She saw no deception in the depths of his velvet-brown eyes, but couldn't believe for a second he thought she was worthy of a date, much less three of them. "We were ten years old." She held out her arms. "You couldn't have been serious." Nell rubbed her forehead. "Were you?"

"Yes, I was." He flashed her a wicked grin, showing his perfect white teeth. "When I was ten, I was a serious kinda guy."

This conversation had taken a turn toward the ridiculous. He had to be pulling her leg. "Riley, that doesn't count."

His grin widened. "I asked you to the Sadie Hawkins dance when you were in eleventh grade."

"You were playing a joke on me." The year before, Avery Prescott, the mayor's son, had asked her to the Winter Cotillion. She'd been excited that a boy her grandmother deemed good enough had actually sought her out and asked her to the formal dance. She'd been given permission to accept, but when the night finally arrived she'd been left standing in her baby-pink formal gown on the porch waiting for a date who had never intended to show up.

He shook his head. "I was serious as a heart attack."

"I guess I was kind of gun-shy. I didn't believe you." She still remembered being devastated, and at school the next Monday, she'd discovered herself the victim of a cruel joke that had left all of her classmates laughing at her. From that time on, she'd hidden herself in her books, worked at the diner and taken care of her grandmother, who grew more delicate every year as her heart grew weaker. She decided she simply wasn't the type of girl men wanted to make time for or go to bed with.

"I also asked you out for dinner about seven months after Chloe and I got divorced and again you turned me down."

"You have dinner at the diner every night." Of course she was always working in a restaurant full of other people waiting for their food and didn't have the kind of time she'd like to spend talking to him. "Why didn't I have a clue?" she asked that question more for herself than him.

"I'm guessing I wasn't clear enough." He leaned

against the kitchen counter. "Why are you asking me to teach you about sex?"

She felt the blush start beneath the collar of her uniform and spread upward again. "All the single women in town you've been running around with say you're the best at…you know…doing it." Not that they'd actually said so directly to her. She'd learned a long time ago that most of the women in Wayloo thought she was invisible and talked freely in front of her when they came to the diner for lunch. But she wisely kept that information to herself. She tended to live vicariously through gossip.

His eyebrows shot up. "They do?"

She nodded, moving closer to him. "I figured you know the tricks. After all, you lived in Chicago for five years. Plus, I don't have to worry about any of the mushy love junk."

"Mushy love junk?"

Okay, maybe she shouldn't have said it exactly that way. It did sound a bit rude and unfeeling. Riley wasn't acting the way she'd envisioned in her mind. She'd thought he'd be…well…more flattered. "I know you're not going to fall in love with me and I'm pretty sure I'm not going to fall in love with you." Almost sure. Deep inside, she'd always had some odd feeling for Riley, but had never really taken it out and examined it. He was just another guy her grandmother had disapproved of, so why waste time on thinking about what-ifs.

"You don't think you could love me?" he asked.

A woman like her would be a fool even to think about setting her sights on such a man as handsome and as eligible as Riley Martin. Since his divorce, the local gossips whispered that he'd been through almost all the single women in the tri-county area. Sex was in his bag of tricks. "It would be silly, since I'm leaving town as soon as I sell the diner and settle all my business. That's why you're so perfect. That and the fact that all the women say you're very good at…well…you know." She just couldn't quite say the word *sex*. She imagined her grandmother sitting on a cloud looking down at her and being horrified at what Nell wanted.

Pride crossed his face. He reminded her of one of her grandmother's prize roosters strutting through the backyard. "I'm flattered I rate town gossip." A frown pulled his face down. "At least, I think I am."

She set her glass of tea down. "I'm starting to believe that this was a very bad idea. I'll be going." She turned to leave, the bitter taste of embarrassment in her mouth. She'd given it a shot and had been shot down.

"Hold on," Riley said.

Nell stopped, knowing she should keep on going, but curiosity was always a demanding thing. And it always seemed to get the better of her at all the wrong times.

"Nell." Riley pushed away from the counter. "I didn't say no."

Nell's breath caught in her throat. "No, I guess

you didn't." He looked so big and solid and his mouth was so soft and inviting. She tried to imagine being kissed by Riley, but all she could remember was Jeremy Hill who'd cornered her in seventh grade and tried to kiss her. His kiss had been wet and totally unromantic.

"No, I didn't." He took a step toward her.

Her head said *leave* one more time, but her feet ignored the command. "Riley, may I ask you a question?"

He hovered over her. "You can ask me anything." His voice had taken on a tone that sent a shiver through Nell.

She looked him straight in the eye. "Why did you ask me to the Sadie Hawkins dance?"

The corner of his mouth tilted up. "Let's call it the lure of the forbidden."

She wasn't sure exactly what he meant, but she certainly wanted to know, if for no other reason than because she got a warm tingly feeling inside her, as if she was doing something really naughty. "I don't understand."

Riley closed the distance between them. "You are the eternal good girl with the hot, sex-kitten body. Why wouldn't I want to go out with you?"

"I'm chubby." She interrupted him. Her grandmother had told her so often enough.

His nostrils flared as his gaze traveled over her body. "Never. Voluptuous, stacked, loaded if you want to get crude. Everything is in all the right places and in the right amounts. But then again, girls like you were always off-limits to bad boys like me."

And he had been a bad boy, riding his old motorcycle around town at all hours of the night with his black leather jacket and that sardonic grin all the girls used to squeal about.

Nell thrilled at his compliment. No one had ever told her such things before. For the first time she felt, well, almost pretty. "My grandmother used to say you'd end up in prison or in a trailer park."

He grinned. "I *was* pretty bad, wasn't I?" A look of pride filled his eyes.

She touched his forearm. His dark skin was corded with the structure of the muscles underneath. Tingles rushed up her fingers. She liked how it felt to connect with him. He was strong, powerful and sturdy, as though he could withstand anything. She hadn't thought physical contact with a man could be so exciting. The hair on the back of her neck rose as a current of electricity danced through her.

"Was, but not anymore." The words came out in a breathy tone she didn't even know she was capable of.

"Well," he said, "I haven't taken a joyride in Mr. Anderson's Pontiac in about ten years."

She felt a laugh struggle to break free. Mr. Anderson had prized his old Pontiac so highly that every high-school boy tried to steal it for a backcountry joyride. Riley had been one of the few to succeed.

In a strange way she wanted to reassure him that

as far as she was concerned he'd proven everyone wrong and she was proud of him. He'd become a nationally respected historical restorationist and had been featured on several PBS shows on historic preservation. The houses he restored were featured in magazines. "But you did something with your life. Something real special."

"Yes, I did."

"And you made some very important contributions to preserving this town's history." Not that she cared about Wayloo's history, but some of the houses were just too pretty to let rot.

"You didn't come here to talk about town history."

"No," she said in a breathless tone. "You're right, I didn't."

His deep velvety voice was doing strange things to her. Things she shouldn't let herself admit. After all, she had been talking to him almost every day for the last few years. Of course, they rarely had conversations outside of the diner. Maybe her grandmother was right. Just the mere mention of the word *sex* made a woman think strange things and want to throw caution to the wind.

"You came to talk about sex." His eyebrows jiggled. "With me."

She wanted to cover her flushed cheeks. She wanted to splash the cool tea all over her face. *Focus,* she admonished herself. *Focus on what you came for, Nell.* "Um, yes."

"Why do you want to know about sex?"

She'd spent her entire life looking at life from the outside. She wasn't going to be the same little mouse in New York she was in Wayloo. She'd be like those women she saw on television and read about in books. In charge of her life, sophisticated and free. "I want to fit in. When I live in the city."

"What else do you want to know?"

His question surprised her. She'd already told him what she wanted.

He moved closer. "Do you want to learn how it feels to touch a man?"

She was tired of reading romances, of reading about women who knew so much more than she did. "Yes."

Riley took another step toward her. "About how it is to kiss a man?"

She could almost feel his body heat. "Yes." Every nerve ached. Despite the air-conditioning her body temperature rose and one side of her brain wondered why and the other side told her to go along with it.

He took another step closer. "And about how to please a man?"

Nell clasped her hands behind her back lest they stray toward him. "Yes."

"Do you know what's going to happen between us?"

She'd watched her share of episodes of *Sex and the City.* She'd read plenty of books. She wasn't totally uneducated. In theory she knew what went on between men and woman. The practical part she understood, she just lacked the experience. "I know the basics." *Don't I sound all worldly and wise?*

He hooked his finger in between two buttons of her uniform at the gap that sometimes showed between her breasts. "Book-learnin' is only going to take a girl so far. We're going to have to sleep together."

She glanced down at his finger. At this moment the polyester was choking her entire body. "I think I can do that." Maybe not. She felt as though she should run away and never come back.

He moved her backward until she felt the edge of the counter pushing against her hips. "Just wanted you to know how it's going to be."

"You'll do it?" A thousand different emotions pushed through her until her breath seemed to stall inside and she grew light-headed.

"Yeah," he replied, "I'll do *it*."

The way he emphasized the word *it* curled her toes. Nell let out a long breath. The last thing on her list completed. "Well, thank you, Riley." She slipped sideways and turned to leave. Not that *leave* was the right word, *escape* was closer in meaning.

Riley grabbed her arm and spun her to face him. "We haven't hashed out the details yet."

Nell bit her lip. "Details?"

Something strange appeared in his eyes that sent a spiral of fire down to her belly so strong she bit her bottom lip. Her breath came in shallow gasps. Her body was so hot she wanted to pour the whole pitcher of cold tea over her head.

Riley pushed her tight against the counter, and she was powerless to stop him, even if she'd really wanted to.

He lowered his head, his mouth touching hers with featherlike gentleness. "Everything important is in the details."

Nell's mouth opened under the insistent pressure of his lips. Time stopped. She felt Riley's hands move up her arms. Heat spiraled outward. Though she understood the biology of love, she didn't understand the pounding wave of anticipation radiating through her.

His tongue slipped between her lips to caress her tongue. Nell's eyes fluttered closed. The bottom of her stomach dropped out of her world. His body molded to hers. His broad chest flattened her breasts. Nell grabbed the fabric of his shirt in her fists. She stood on tiptoes and opened her mouth wider. Her first real kiss. The kind of kiss an adult man gave an adult woman. Nothing could have been more perfect.

His long, callused fingers climbed up her shoulders and locked behind her neck. The tips of his thumbs caressed her chin. Heat, desire, need overwhelmed her. She couldn't seem to catch her breath. She didn't want the moment to end. Her nipples tightened in her too-restrictive bra. She wanted to free her breasts, to touch his bare skin. She knew this was bad, but everything felt so right. Her grandmother had lied. His touch was sheer heaven.

Then Riley lifted his head.

Nell couldn't breathe as she stared into his dark eyes and saw her own startled-doe look reflected back at her. He looked at her as if she were the most beautiful woman in the world.

His mouth tilted into a wicked smile. "I believe we've worked out the first detail."

Nell wanted to touch the spot he'd kissed to capture the hot memory in her hand and keep it forever. "What's that?"

"To see whether we have chemistry."

She couldn't relax, couldn't make the heat inside her leave. "Do we?"

He grinned. "Oh yeah."

Good, she thought. Now there was only one question left for her to ask. "When do we get started?"

Chapter 3

Riley picked at his lonely plate of spaghetti. After Nell had dropped her bombshell, he was surprised he'd still ended up alone tonight. Well, maybe that was a good thing. Tomorrow evening would be soon enough to start her education. Hell, he was probably in for a few new things himself.

His head was still reeling. In a short time his boyhood fantasy was about to come true. Nell, naked and willing in his bed. He raised his eyes to Heaven. *Thank you, God.* He twirled the tomato-paste-covered noodles on his fork. As he lifted the fork he heard a knock on the back door. A second later the door opened. Only one person walked into his house this way—his ex-wife Chloe.

"Riley Francis Martin, what the hell is going on?" The back door slammed and the stained-glass panels rattled.

Gritting his teeth, he waited for the sound of antique glass to hit the handmade Italian marble he'd laid there three weeks ago. "Hello to you, too, Chloe." He heard her high heels click on the hardwood hallway floor as she made her way to the den. He took a quick look around the room, even though he knew there was nowhere to hide.

He knew her moods, and he felt that he was in for one now.

Riley put down the fork and picked up the television remote control, fighting the urge to hit the volume control to turn up the sound and tune her out, but that wasn't going to be a safe option. Reluctantly he turned off the Braves baseball game he wasn't watching anyway and waited to hear from his ex, or, as he sometimes like to call her, the Harbinger of Doom.

Chester gave a low whine, then got up from his doggy bed in the corner and slunk out of the room like the coward he was. His toenails clicked on the floor as he ran out of the den. Chloe and Chester had never been the best of friends even on a good day.

Chloe tapped her way into the den and leaned over his TV tray, gripping the edges tightly. Her dark brown hair swung along the crest of her shoulders. Her pale brown eyes blazed at him. "And just what in the ever-lovin' hell has gotten into your head?"

Riley shrugged and pointed to the television. "Watching the game and eating dinner."

Her eyes narrowed. "You know what I mean."

Guess that wasn't the answer she wanted. "Actually, no I don't." When in doubt, go for dumb.

Her long red fingernails tapped on the TV tray. "Why are you are turning Nell Evans into your personal sex puppet?"

Okay, now he knew what had gotten her knickers into a twist. He sat back in his chair, knowing he was in trouble and wanting to get out of face-slapping distance. Chloe had never hit him during their marriage, but there was always a first time—and he was pretty sure she was close to reaching her boiling point. "How did you find out?"

Chloe straightened up and flipped her hair back. "Nell told me everything."

Riley cringed, his stomach roiling This was not good. "She did?"

"She even asked me to go shopping with her in New Orleans. She wants the works. A new wardrobe, a new hairstyle and a new face."

Oh, God! How could Nell tell his ex-wife? "She really told you?"

Chloe crossed her arms and tapped her fingers on her arms. "When a girl like Nell decides to get herself a new image, there is a reason behind it besides falling into a lot of money. I weaseled an explanation out of her. One that would curl the hair of the most jaded of people."

You mean you got out the velvet-covered rubber hoses, he thought. When she wanted info, Chloe could be merciless. "You didn't hurt her, did you?"

She sneered at him. "That would be worse than kicking a puppy."

Maybe so, but Chloe was going to ruin Nell. He could just picture her in makeup, fake nails and dyed hair. Not that Chloe wasn't one of the most beautiful women in the universe, but Nell was perfect the way she was. He didn't want another beauty queen, he wanted Nell. "Don't help her. Please. I like her the way she is."

"She wouldn't take no for an answer." She spread her arms in a dramatic gesture. "She thinks I can help her craft a whole new sophisticated image for the Big Apple. She said spare no expense. How could I turn down something like that?"

Yeah, so she can look sexy for some other guy. That didn't sit well with him. "Damn."

Now the hands went to her hips. "Don't you dare hurt her. She's not like your usual women. She doesn't understand the rules of the game."

Not his rules. Nell seemed to be playing by her own set of rules. Rules he was willing to play by for one taste of her sweetness. Rules he'd bend in a heartbeat. Hell, he'd run naked down Main Street coated in honey and pickle juice if she wanted him to. "Chloe, she came to me for help. How could I turn down an offer like that?"

"She is like a woman possessed." Chloe paced the den, then stopped and stared at him.

"Tell me about it," he agreed.

"I think she wanted to ask about the intimate details of our marriage."

Pain shot through his head like a bullet. He pinched the bridge of his nose. What had he gotten himself into? "Don't say anything about how things were between us."

A sly grin appeared on her full red lips. "Trust me, your secrets are safe with me. Nobody would believe me anyway."

He might have started out that way, but once he understood the game and learned all about peak performance, his abilities had improved tremendously. "Gee, thanks."

"Grow up, Riley." She sat down. "Why did you agree to this?"

Now, how did he tell his ex-wife about fantasies over another woman that had been in his head since he'd formally been introduced to his hormones? Despite all the things that had gone wrong between them, he and Chloe had never lied to each other about anything. They'd married because Chloe had gotten pregnant with Benjy. They'd had a good marriage as marriages go, but it had been built on their son, not on love for each other. "It just sort of came up."

Chloe rubbed her eyes. "I can ask this because we have a lot of history together, and we're better together as friends than we ever were as husband and wife. You have always secretly lusted after Nell, haven't you?"

Chloe had the wonderful gift of being able to cut through the bullshit, no matter what. He'd always figured he'd hidden his Nell-lusting pretty well. He'd been faithful to Chloe no matter what he might have wanted to do. That was what real men did, but what did a man say in a situation like this? Denial was right there on his tongue. "Well…"

Chloe held up her hand. "You don't have to spare my feelings. Honey, I've seen the way you stare at Nell sometimes. Half the time you could trip over your tongue like a lovesick boy. She's a sweet, beautiful woman. You could do a lot worse. I don't know how you're going to let her go when she's done with you."

"She's not really looking for forever. And neither am I. I'm not good at long-term anymore. If I was I'd still be your husband."

Chloe suddenly looked sad as old memories filled her eyes. "I know if Benjy hadn't died we'd still be together. I never deluded myself about our relationship. Neither did you. We made the best out of a confusing situation. When the unthinkable happened, we didn't have enough love for each other to keep the bitterness away. Maybe if we'd had other children we could have kept going. I'm not good at living in the past, I like to keep moving forward."

"You think your being so understanding makes me feel better? I can't…I wish…" He floundered for words. Pain still raged through him. Pain that never seemed to leave him or lessen. He could go on with everyday life but, damn, the raw hurt never went away. "I should have been...I didn't know how to be there for you. You were so—"

She shook her head. "I didn't know how to be there for you either. No one is at fault. Passion is a great thing, and we had that to spare. But it wasn't enough to keep us together. Stop letting his death eat you up. You're still alive. He was killed by a drunk driver. We did everything right. We had him for four years. That's more than a lot of people get." Tears filled her eyes and she impatiently brushed them away with the back of her hand.

He knew she was right, but letting himself not feel beyond the surface seemed safer. He wasn't like her. She had a lot in her heart. Every bit he had was taken up by his son. And when Benjy had died, he'd closed himself off to everything. "How come you're the smart one?"

She dropped her fist on his knee. "I'm an ex-beauty queen. All that mascara stimulated my brain cells."

"Oh yeah, I forgot."

As she stood, she wiped a tear away from her cheek. "If you hurt Nell, I promise I'll gut you." Her chin went up. "And I won't be quick about it."

He had no doubt Chloe meant every word. He didn't want to hurt Nell. As she'd said, damaging Nell would be worse than kicking a puppy—it would be stomping the poor thing in the head. "Nell is safe with me."

"Be ready at nine on Saturday morning. You are going to the land of the enemy."

A sharp, cold chill ran up his spine, and he could smell his own fear. He had never gone shopping with Chloe when they'd been married and he sure as shit wasn't about to go now they were divorced. "What do I know about women's clothes?" Okay, he was good at getting them off. And paying for them. That was the extent of his expertise and he planned to keep it that way.

"Trust me. You know plenty." She hooked a thumb toward his bulging magazine rack in the corner next to Chester's bed. "And don't try and hoodwink me, I know you have your own subscription to the Victoria's Secret catalog."

I'm so busted. He hoped he looked a little bit ashamed, but he didn't think so. "That may be so, but I'm still not going with you."

"You damn well *are* coming. I'm not the one she's hoping to impress. I'm not about to make over your sex puppet all by myself." She smiled. "I'm not that good."

What the hell did he know about dressing a woman. "I don't know about that crap. Take Mario." Mario, an old high-school friend of them both, owned a fashion boutique the next town over.

"You are a straight man. You know what other straight men like. Mario is wonderful, but given no firm direction, he'll dress the poor thing like a drag queen. I want your help on the clothes."

"Damn. I knew this was going to get way too complicated."

Chloe leaned on the doorjamb and crossed her arms. "I should have figured out long ago why you liked me to dress up as a waitress, as opposed to a French maid or a candy striper."

He was a guy, what did she expect? The heat of embarrassment crept up his face. The naughty waitress was his favorite fantasy. "I plead the fifth."

She pursed her lips. "I didn't make the connection until after our divorce when you started hanging around the diner every day for lunch and dinner. But there is one good thing about this."

"What?"

Pushing away from the doorway she shrugged. "At least you never called me by her name."

She had always been a woman who could be direct no matter if she hurt his feelings. But that statement was particularly low. "That's cold, Chloe."

"I call it like I see it." She saluted him. "And we're taking your Escalade. I'm driving. You'd better have it detailed." She whirled around and tapped her way toward the back door.

Chloe was right, he did get to have one of his major sex fantasies fulfilled, although he didn't want to think about making sweet virginal Nell into his personal sex puppet. Especially since she planned to take her act on the road. Somehow the thought of her leaving so soon was not sitting well with him.

Sitting back in his easy chair, he swallowed the acid in his throat.

Nell had been surprised when the phone rang and Riley had called to say he would be right over. When they had parted earlier in the day, she'd thought he would take some time to really think about her offer, but here he was on his way.

She'd taken a quick shower, put on her prettiest skirt and white cotton blouse, then rushed around the living room straightening pillows and pushing a feather duster over every little knickknack and her grandmother's antique clock on the mantel over the fireplace. Her grandmother had loved the clock and for a second Nell felt a storm of tears brewing at the sides of her eyes. She wouldn't cry, not anymore. She needed to move forward.

She heard Riley's car pull up into the driveway. She gave herself one last look in the mirror as she tossed the feather duster into a drawer. From the drawer, she pulled out a small spiral-bound notebook and pen and set it where she could easily find it. She'd bought the notebook at Doolittle's after she'd left Riley. If she was going to learn so many new things, she needed to take notes.

The doorbell rang and Nell checked her breath and then opened the door to find him leaning against the jamb looking so masculine he sent heat racing through her like a summer thunderstorm. Her heart pounded at the look in his face and she stood aside to let him in.

Riley walked in looking big and male and out of place among her grandmother's dark wood furniture. His sheer masculinity just made everything smaller. Nell felt as if she were violating some sacred temple as she looked around her grandmother's small tidy house and tried not to think about what she and Riley were about to do. But Riley had insisted that she would be more comfortable in her territory.

The black shirt and tight jeans fitted over every muscle of his body. Her heart fluttered. She wished she didn't feel so anxious.

Sex was a biological function like breathing or eating, right? What was the great mystery? Wiping her damp palms on her yellow-and-black floral skirt, she took a deep calming breath. The less nervous she was the more likely she was going to be a better student.

She'd only admit it to herself, but he could take her breath away like no other man ever could. In a way, he was what she always thought a real man should be. Clean, strong and a bit rough around the edges—everything her grandmother had warned her about for years. Where these bad-girl thoughts had come from was a mystery to her. All she knew for certain was that she wanted to be very, very bad. With Riley. "What should we start with?"

The corner of his mouth went up. "Touching. Men love to be touched."

Her bottom lip trembled. She could think of nothing else but the kiss she and Riley had shared. She hadn't expected the kiss to be so intense or so passionate. Her nerves tingled with anticipation. He took her hand and placed it on his chest. Slowly she touched him, feeling the hardness of his muscles, the heat of his skin, the texture of the cotton shirt.

She could feel him breathing, his broad chest rising and falling. Until now she'd never thought of a man's body as a thing of beauty, but Riley was glorious. The tip of her finger grazed the fabric of his shirt and her throat went dry. Her hand began to tremble.

She was so excited. She felt so naughty and wicked and almost immoral. She tried not to think about Pastor Willis and his sermons. She was about to do everything her grandmother and Pastor Willis had warned her was bad.

"Come on, Nell," Riley said softly, "you can do better than this."

She licked her dry bottom lip, but didn't proceed any further. She was too afraid to do the wrong thing. "I don't know how."

Riley gripped her wrist. "Let me show you." He forced her hand flat against the wall of his chest and covered her hand with his.

His strong, callused fingers were rough on her hot skin. The longer he held on the more she wanted. She placed the other hand on his chest, right over his heart. Under her hand, his heart raced.

He took a sharp breath.

Feeling a sense of freedom, she let herself explore him. "I've never seen a naked man before." Did those words really come out of her mouth? Her voice sounded strange.

"Don't you have Internet?" he asked.

She did now. She'd had DSL put in the week after her grandmother had passed. "Well yes, but, you know, the FBI can track where you've been on those sites and I don't want that on my record." Somehow her grandmother would have found out.

He chuckled. "We'll have to change that, won't we?"

His low seductive laugh rolled over her, curling her toes. Nell clenched her knees together to stop their shaking. She didn't think he was asking a question. Nor did she care. "Yes. Please."

He lowered her hands to her side. Then he started to unbutton his shirt.

This wasn't how she wanted to do this. She wanted to undress him herself and discover his body in her own way. Nell grabbed his wrists. His muscles flexed under her hand. "No, I want to undress you." As soon as the words left her mouth, she was shocked that she'd said them.

Riley raised an eyebrow. "I'd like that."

She couldn't help herself, she giggled. "Do most men like a woman undressing them?"

"I like a woman who lets me know what she wants."

"Why?"

"Because that means they're as excited about going to bed with you as you are about them."

Okay, she thought, *I can do that.* Nell let go of his wrists. His hands dropped to his sides. Her stomach fluttered with excitement and anticipation. There was a languid achy feeling between her thighs. She was a bit disconcerted about her body's reactions. To go from zero to red-hot inferno had to be bad. But she didn't care. One part of her felt as if she was abandoning everything her grandmother had taught her about what was proper. She'd heard the stories of her mother's too-easy reputation and tried all her life to be different from that. Deep down inside, maybe she was more like her mother than she believed she was. The thought didn't make her feel naughty as she suspected it would. "You're shaking."

"I'm excited."

"Me, too." Nell freed the top button of his shirt. His skin was a smooth earthy bronze color. He was warm and alive. The aching in her body became more fierce as she unfastened the next button.

"Nell, before we go any further, I want to make one thing perfectly clear to you."

That this was real. She already knew that. "What?"

"If at any time you want to stop, we stop."

He didn't have to say that. She knew she could trust him with her body. "I know."

"Not just with me, but with any man. Promise me you won't waste your time on a man you can't trust." He reached up and touched her cheek.

Nell rubbed her face against his palm. She drew from his strength. He knew how to comfort a woman and make her feel safe. "I promise."

Nell undid another button and pulled the hem of his shirt out of his jeans. She pushed the fabric aside to reveal his wide shoulders. He shrugged out of the shirt and she leaned back to look at the smooth expanse of his chest. He was beautiful. The shirt dropped from her cold fingers to the rug, landing near his feet.

She raised her eyes to him again, and saw that his entire body was sculpted like a Greek statue, all corded muscles and six-pack abs. His skin was smooth and a rich cinnamon-brown that made her gasp. No statue, he was alive and hot, not cold marble. His chest rose and fell with every breath. His nipples, small and brown, were like hard pebbles. Carefully she reached up and touched one nipple with the tip of her finger.

Riley sucked in a quick breath and Nell felt a surge of power. This was better than unwrapping her presents on Christmas morning. Nell glanced down at the telltale bulge in his jeans. Pride swelled inside her. She, plain old Nell, could make a man feel desire.

Riley leaned forward until his mouth was less than an inch from her ear. "That's what you do to me, Nell. What you've always done to me."

She met his smoldering gaze, silently thanking

him, but not sure if she completely believed him. "I want to see you naked."

His mouth curved into a smile. "You say the sweetest things."

She'd never felt so bold in all her life. Something about the twinkle in his eyes, the wicked smile that just made her feel so darn comfortable and more importantly…confident. "You make me feel very naughty." Naughty and wicked and any number of things. She hoped her grandmother wasn't sitting on a cloud looking down and watching her.

"Good for me." He ran a hand up her arm to her neck and the line of her jaw.

She wanted to purr. The feel of his fingers on her skin sent a shiver through her that made her want to curl her toes and fall back on the sofa. Her hands went to the waistband of his jeans. "I didn't think I'd ever be so bold." Not with any man. So few men had ever been in her life.

He started laughing.

"What's so funny?" she asked impatiently.

He looked down at his feet. "I'm just really glad I took off my socks and shoes."

She opened her mouth to ask why.

Riley winked at her. "It will make it easier for you to get my pants off."

She covered her smiling mouth with her fingers, refusing to be shocked. Refusing to let all her grandmother's rules about dates and men rush through her head. Flinging caution to the wind, she ran a questing finger across the round bulge of his jeans. "I see what you mean."

"Come on, Nell. Take off my pants. See what you do to me."

The metal button on his jeans gave her a little resistance, but she finally managed to unbutton it. The jeans fell open and she slipped her hands inside the waistband to caress the smooth skin of his hips. He wasn't wearing any underwear. How very improper—and so very sexy.

She thought of her own little-old-lady underwear—cotton panties and a plain cotton bra. She'd have to get new sexy lingerie when she went shopping with Chloe on Saturday. For a second her mind wandered at the thought of sexy fire engine-red thong panties and a matching bra of smooth satin. Maybe blue would be better; she wasn't a "red" type of girl.

She didn't realize she'd stopped stroking him until he covered her hand with his.

"Don't stop now," he said, his breath coming out in a rush. "I'm enjoying myself."

"Really?"

"You have very soft hands. I like being this close to you, too. You smell good."

"Cotton blossom lotion." Her grandmother had given her a selection of lotions, soaps and perfumes over the years and she'd always been saving them for when she'd need them. Tonight, she knew, was the time to crack the seals on those bottles. "I didn't want to smell like chicken-fried steak, but you probably don't want to know that, do you?"

"Chicken-fried steak isn't so bad, but I'm pleased you went with cotton blossom. I like a lot of things about you." He gently nibbled at her ear.

Heat started in her nipples and spread in ever-widening circles around her breasts. "Thank you for doing this for me."

He pushed a stray tendril off her cheek. "Trust me, it's my pleasure."

His low, seductive voice rolled over her. The deep tones stirred her senses. "Not just the sex part, but for making me feel beautiful. Wanted." For making her feel like a real woman.

"You *are* beautiful."

She didn't quite believe him, as much as she wanted to. "I'm nervous I'll do the wrong thing."

"Just keep doing what you're doing."

"I want…" *Don't get shy now, Nell,* she chided herself. "I want to do more." Deep inside her a feeling she didn't recognize grew and grew.

He guided her hand. "That's good." The corner of his mouth lifted.

His words were barely more than a whisper, but they echoed through her head. Nell took a deep breath. She closed her eyes and pushed his jeans down, feeling her knuckles skim across his hips, his thighs, and when she reached his ankles she stood, but didn't open her eyes. She was so frightened and excited she wasn't sure if she could speak.

"Look at me, Nell." Riley's voice sounded tight and hoarse.

She opened one eye. She was level with his smiling mouth. She opened the other eye, and let her gaze roam down to his strong chin. Then to the corded muscles in his neck. She studied the wide set of his muscular shoulders. He had a little scar just beneath his collarbone and she wondered what had happened. She found another little scar in the crook of his elbow. She glanced down and spied the tip of his erect penis. She bit her bottom lip. Oh! He was so big.

Riley dragged one foot out of his pants then the other, then he kicked them aside. "Touch me, Nell."

"Where?"

"Anywhere you want. Everywhere you want."

Nell reached and pressed her hand flat against his chest. She was going to have to work up to touching his penis. Living, breathing muscle contracted under her hand.

She put her other hand on his shoulder. She moved closer and planted a kiss right on his heart. He groaned. Nell felt power radiating from him. She moved her lips over his smooth skin. "You are so beautiful," she murmured.

"Thank you." He pulled her close to him, pressing her tightly to his chest. He kissed her, his lips soft, his tongue hard.

Nell felt his penis pressing into her through the light cotton material of her skirt. The moist heat stunned her. A flood of emotions raged inside her. Finally, she thought, she would know what other women knew, feel what other women felt.

Nell's hands roamed over his body. She licked his skin, loving the salty taste of him. Riley trembled as she ran her fingers down the smooth skin of his back and then around his hips to the heat of his penis. She loved the feel of the smoothness in her hand. In all her life, she'd dreamed and wondered what a man felt like, and the reality exceeded all her dreams.

Nell giggled, feeling wanton and feminine. Had she known this would be so intoxicating, she would have found a man a long ago time, despite her grandmother's warnings that men weren't to be trusted.

She wanted to touch Riley everywhere. With her bottom lip caught between her teeth, she reached out and touched the tip of his hard penis and jerked back, surprised. The skin was velvety hot and silky smooth and slightly moist. As she curled her hand around him and stroked from base to tip, a moaning sigh escaped his lips. What had she been missing? Apparently a whole lot.

She wasn't certain what she'd expected, but she found herself thinking about the sex education classes she'd had, and she realized how inadequate they had been. The classes had not even prepared her for the most basic of her emotions. The clinical aspect of sex was one thing, but the reality was far different.

She cupped him in both hands, running her palms

down the sides. His penis seemed to jerk in her hand
as if it had a mind of its own.

This is what women yearned for. She wrapped her
fingers around him. Her eyes closed as she tried to
imagine them making love, him on top of her, being
touched by him, invaded by him. Her mouth opened,
her breathing became labored.

"Nell?"

She looked up at him, letting go of his penis. "Am
I doing something wrong?"

"The doorbell."

She looked toward the front door. It might be
rude, but she wasn't home.

Before he could respond, the doorbell rang again.
"Don't answer," he said, his voice harsh.

She smiled at him. "I don't intend to." Not for
anything would she interrupt this session. If it was
another floral arrangement from someone in town,
the florist could leave the arrangement. If it was
someone else, that person could come back when
they realized she wasn't going to answer.

The front door crashed open. "Hello?"

Nell froze with her fingers still wrapped around
Riley's penis.

"Nell, honey," came a once-familiar trilling voice.
"It's Mama. I'm home."

Chapter 4

Speechless, Nell stared at her mother. Lucy Evans stood in the entry, her eyes going wide first with surprise, then disbelief and finally mischief.

Lucy dropped her suitcase on the floor. The dull thud reverberated through the silent house. "Nell, honey, whatever is going on here?" Her dark eyes raked over Riley who, after a paralyzed moment, scooped his pants up off the floor and held them in front of him. "Or do I want to know?"

Sliding a glance at Riley, Nell noticed he'd hidden that wonderful part of himself that most intrigued her and that she'd so enjoyed touching. Her fingers still ached to touch him, but not with her mama standing in the doorway and staring at her with that all-knowing expression on her incredibly beautiful face.

The first thought into her head sent shame through her. Nell's greatest fear had just happened, she had become just like her mother.

"Mama, what are you doing here?" Nell stepped in front of Riley to shield him from Lucy's questioning gaze, giving him a chance to put his clothes back on. Her own clothes felt way too tight, but at least they were still on.

"I'm visiting," Lucy replied.

The words sank in as Nell stared at her mother.

Lucy Evans hadn't changed since Nell had last seen her over seven years ago. Her slender, petite body was as delicate as ever. Not one wrinkle marred her high-cheekboned face and her flawless, bronze-tinted skin glowed with vitality and health. Her eyes were large and tilted up slightly at the outer corners, her nose was straight and her mouth wide and generous.

Lucy Evans was the most beautiful woman Nell had ever known, with the kind of sensual allure prized by modeling agencies and movie producers. She was perfection, with her black hair flowing smoothly about her shoulders and the way she moved with such fluid, elegant grace. She was the kind of woman who could wear a potato sack and make it look like high-end fashion. She was the kind of woman Nell would never be.

"Oh." Nell straightened her clothes, mad at herself that *oh* was the only word she could think to say.

She began feeling unattractive again. Her mother always made her feel dowdy and undignified. Nell was a mud hen, brown and nondescript, next to Lucy, the awe-inspiring peacock.

Riley struggled into his pants and zipped them up, his eyes rolling just a little when he hit a sensitive spot. "Miz Lucy," he said politely, though his voice was strained and tight. "How are you?"

Lucy gave him an up-and-down look. "I'm fine, Riley, considerin' everything," Lucy replied in a cool, amused voice. Her sharp gaze flicked over him, taking in his bare chest and tight jeans. "But I have to admit, I'm a bit surprised to see you here, playing fast and loose with my little girl." She gave a flirtatious little giggle and a knowing smile.

Nell felt two inches tall. She tried to hide her embarrassment, but her only defense was to look away.

Lucy Evans tended to blow in and out of Nell's life like a Texas thunderstorm, leaving behind chaos and anger. And here she was back again to wreak her special brand of bedlam just like the seven-year locusts.

"What are you doing here?" Nell asked as she racked her brain on how to get rid of her mama. Lucy had been walking in and out of Nell's life since she could remember. And nothing good ever seemed to come from it.

"I just heard about my mama." Lucy walked over and pulled Nell into her arms and patted her hard on the back. "I just can't believe she's really dead. I always thought the old girl was indestructible."

Nell clamped her mouth shut before something truly ugly flew out. The grief she kept at bay threatened to push beyond the walls she'd built, but she fought to keep her heartache contained. With Lucy, she couldn't afford to lose her focus.

Lucy broke away with a shrewd glance at Nell. "I tell ya what, seeing as you two have some unfinished business, I'll just take my luggage upstairs and get unpacked." She kissed Nell on the tip of her nose. Her touch was as brief and light as a butterfly. "Come talk to me when you're done." And then she winked before prancing back to her luggage.

Nell felt Riley at her back as he watched Lucy. "Miz Lucy," he drawled, "I'll take your luggage up." Ever the polite Southern gentleman.

Lucy dimpled at him, her delicate hands fluttering. "Aren't you a sweetie? But I can see y'all are busy." She tapped Nell on the cheek. "I'll be fine. Y'all just go right on doing what y'all were doin'." She winked at Nell and waltzed back through the front door and dragged her other suitcases in.

"I'm sorry, Riley," Nell said after her mother had traipsed up the stairs. She tried to control her runaway emotions and keep the awful ache in her middle from exploding. She'd come so close to losing herself in him, and the memory of his smooth skin under her fingers sent her pulse racing. Now her mother had to show up and ruin everything just as she always did.

Riley pulled Nell into his arms. "We'll continue

this at a later date." He kissed her, his mouth open and exploring, his tongue tangling with hers. Nell almost melted with the strength of her desire.

Pushing that desperate feeling in her stomach down, Nell tried to smile. "Promise?"

"Oh yeah," he said, touching the tip of her nose with his finger. He pulled on his shoes and grabbed his shirt on the way out the door, and not until he was at the door and looking back at her with a look she couldn't interpret did she realize how he brought her grandmother's house to life.

Nell wrapped her arms around her middle, still not sure if she believed him. "I understand if you—"

"I always keep my promises," he interrupted her just before he turned and headed out into the night.

Nell stood in the center of the living room listening to the sound of his car. She looked at the stairs leading to the second floor wishing she could put off the family reunion. A wave of foreboding washed over her as she wondered what she was going to do with her mother.

Lucy Evans was one of the big mysteries in Nell's life. Always lingering in the background, but never really a part of her life.

Nell sighed as she walked up the stairs, down the hall to the bedroom her mother always occupied when she visited.

Lucy sat on the bed in her old bedroom, her legs crossed and a cigarette lighter in her hands. She flicked open the lighter and lit the cigarette dangling between her lips.

Nell snatched the cigarette out of Lucy's mouth. "There is no smoking in my grandmother's house," she snarled and crumpled the cigarette in her fist, then threw it in a small trash can next to the night table.

Lucy's eyes went wide. "My goodness, the little kitten has claws after all. Who'd have thunk it?"

Nell stared at her mother, not knowing how to answer. "Why are you here?" She tried to sound cordial, but her tone was strained.

"Sugar," Lucy said with a tremor in her voice, "I came back to say a proper goodbye to my mama. You can't be all by yourself now, grieving and all. I know you two were close. I thought you might be lonely. And I really just wanted to see you."

Yeah right, Nell thought, her thoughts skittering around. "What do you know?"

"That it was sudden and you already had the funeral without me."

Staring at her mother sitting on the double bed, Nell searched for signs of guile in her face, but she didn't see any. Which confused her to no end. Usually her mother came back home with an agenda. An agenda Nell usually had no trouble figuring out. It had to be the money. She wanted her share. "Why didn't you come to the funeral?"

Lucy stuffed the lighter back into her black leather purse. "I've been in the Bahamas working for the last three months and I just got back. I had major postal issues and didn't find out she'd died until yesterday. As soon as I read the letter from Billy Ray, I hopped a plane and here I am." She spread her arms wide. "I just can't let you go through this difficult time all by yourself, baby."

Nell snorted. *Gee thanks.* "The funeral was three weeks ago. I've already gone through this difficult time all by myself, Mama."

Her mother took a big breath and smiled. "But, sugah, I came as soon as I heard."

Nell folded her arms over her chest. Her gut feeling was her mother wasn't lying, but that didn't mean Nell was going to let her guard down. Eighteen-point-five million dollars was a lot of money to go around and it brought out the worst in people, even people Nell had known all her life. Though she felt badly thinking about Lucy's greed, one thing Nell wasn't, was a fool. "I really am fine."

Lucy winked. "I can see that. Riley Martin in the living room completely undressed. And who knows what else is going on. I am surprised. My baby seems to be growing up at last."

"I haven't been a baby in a very long time." As if Lucy even cared. She'd dropped Nell off when she had been a baby, appearing now and again during Nell's life, and never once had she asked Nell how she was going on. "I don't think I need any advice from you."

"Is that why Riley was buck-naked in your

grandmama's living room doing things we don't need to mention?"

"I'm twenty-five years old." And she knew exactly what she'd been doing. If Lucy hadn't arrived, she'd have done a whole lot more.

Lucy folded her arms across her chest. "And Riley Martin knows exactly how to plan an assault on a sweet woman like you."

"A sweet woman like me!" Nell was incredulous. "You don't know who I am."

An odd look passed across Lucy's face. "And I take the blame for that." She bit her lip. Nell saw regret and hurt in her mother's eyes and didn't understand. "But there are a lot of things I want to share with you."

That was a cryptic response and Nell didn't want to know what had prompted it or even to know anything more about her mother's life than she already did. *Hell, why should I care?*

"But," Lucy said, examining her long, red fingernails, "that is a conversation for another time. How long have you been seeing Riley?"

Nell didn't have a ready answer. "Not long." Less than a day, but Lucy didn't need to know.

Lucy gave Nell another searching look. "And he likes you?"

In a defensive tone, Nell said, "Maybe he likes me because I'm nice, kind and smart. Maybe Riley is one of those people who just understands what a woman needs. He doesn't need my money, if that's what you're implying. He does very well for himself."

"I didn't ask *why* he's seeing you, I just wanted to know how long you two have been dating?"

"I already told you," Nell said, staring hard at her mother for whom, according to Grandmama, time had never been a prerequisite for a relationship. Nell put her hands on her hips, prepared to defend Riley passionately. "Riley is a well-known architect and historical preservationist. His services are in demand all over the South. People come to him to have their homes restored to what they were originally. He knows more about..." She stopped defending him in the face of her mother's disbelief. "People can change, you know." Everyone, that is, except her mother. Lucy was still self-involved. She would never change.

"Yes, I know that, sugah. Everybody can change, if they want to."

What was her mother trying to tell her? Nell stared at her, unbelieving. What she really wanted to do was tell Lucy she could spend the night but in the morning she needed to get herself over to Chloe's Bed-and-Breakfast, but Nell couldn't. Despite her mother's ways, she was still family and no matter what or who they were, family was important.

She felt a little irritated with herself for being so spineless. "I'll let you get yourself unpacked. Good night, Mama."

Nell stomped out, feeling as though she'd been outmaneuvered and went down to the kitchen to fix herself a snack.

* * *

Cold water pelted Riley's skin. This erotic tutorial with Nell was going to be the death of him. He leaned his head against the slick wet tiles of his shower. What had started out as just a "kissing lesson" had turned into something he'd never be able to turn off.

He'd been in the shower for over thirty minutes and his body still ached for fulfillment. If not for Lucy barging in like a steamroller, he'd have had Nell exactly where he wanted her. Naked, on her back, with him buried deep inside her.

Since she'd gotten him out of his pants, he couldn't stop thinking that maybe agreeing to the sex lesson wasn't his best idea. On paper, the idea had seemed like a gift from the gods. But in actuality the plan wasn't going his way. Oh, he'd get to sleep with Nell, but getting to that point was going to be hell with her mother back around.

Plus he had to take things slow, he didn't want to spook Nell. He wanted her to be as ready for him as he was for her. He wanted to show her that sex was more than just heavy panting and carnal knowledge. He wanted to show her the romance as well.

The thought of her taking all the things they'd share and getting some other guy bothered him. Not that he wanted anything permanent. He couldn't do forever again. He and Chloe had already given it their best shot and failed. No, he didn't have room in his heart for a lifetime kind of love. When Benjy had died, he hadn't thought he'd ever recover. He just went on with his day-to-day life, but something was missing. What Nell wanted from him was about all he was capable of giving.

Riley turned off the water and stepped out of the shower. Chester was sitting outside the shower stall whining. Guess the old boy must have been attuned to his mood.

Riley toweled himself off and dressed quickly. He still had some sexual energy to work off so he took Chester out for a long walk. As he and Chester strolled through the dark, quiet streets, Riley couldn't seem to get Nell out of his thoughts.

The next morning, Riley almost raced out of the house in his eagerness to see Nell. Even though she was now a wealthy woman, she had decided to continue working at the diner until she sold it. Riley didn't know why she wanted to keep working, but he liked that she didn't intend to change her life too much. At least not yet.

The diner sat on a corner of the two-block-long downtown area of Wayloo. The sign, Granny's Diner, was attached to the facade over the door and hadn't been changed in fifty years. Inside, the diner was all chrome and red vinyl with black and white linoleum tiles on the floor. A fifties icon, the diner had the best food in Wayloo. Almost the only food in Wayloo.

The morning crowd was larger than normal. Nell

worked the counter and as Riley entered, he saw that every stool was filled and he had no place to sit. He always sat at Nell's station on the next to last seat near the pie display and his spot was filled.

Every unmarried, unattached male in Wayloo sat at the counter gazing adoringly at Nell. Nell lifted her head and Riley could see she was frowning. When she saw him, she smiled and then turned around to grab a coffeepot.

A sense of panic filled him. Where was he going to eat? He thought about leaving until he spotted Chloe, sitting all by herself in a booth near the back. She lifted a hand and beckoned Riley over.

Riley slid into the booth. "What the hell is going on here? Floyd Beckham is sitting in my spot at Nell's station and we have to sit—" he glanced around "—at Dee Dee's station." Dee Dee was the sexiest waitress at the diner and usually all the unmarried guys sat at her station hoping one of her silicone boobs would slip out of her uniform and say howdy to the fellas. All the married men sat at Nell's station because they liked the service she gave and it didn't tick off their wives.

"You sound like you're five years old and having a temper tantrum," Chloe chided as she sipped her coffee. "Get over yourself."

He gave his stool another forlorn glance. "But that's my seat," Riley complained. "I sit there every morning, have a cup of coffee and a Spanish omelet, and read the sports page. That's how I start my

morning. How I like starting my morning. Floyd,
Jasper and Earl are supposed to be sitting here in Dee
Dee's station placing bets on how badly she screws
up their orders, and hoping she'll give them a nipple
slip."

Chloe burst out laughing. "Obviously, you have
to get up earlier." She pointed over to the corner
table and he saw seven bouquets of flowers and as
many wrapped candy boxes piled to one side.
"Honey, rich is the new sexy. And you have to be
smarter than the competition."

"She's not going to fall for all that fake interest,
is she?" Riley slid a glance at Nell.

Nell looked harried with tendrils of black hair
flying about her head as she slapped plates down on
the counter and poured coffee. Tucker Kittridge
leaned toward her as though to whisper in her ear, but
she brushed him away as though he were nothing
more than an annoying fly and stalked toward the
pass-through to the kitchen to pick up plates she
balanced on her arms. She almost flung the plates at
the men at the counter, irritation in her brown eyes
even though she smiled. If her teeth were tightly
clenched, no one seemed to notice—or didn't want to.

"Sit back and enjoy the show," Chloe said.

"She's mine," Riley growled.

Chloe raised her elegant eyebrows. "Excuse me?"

He pointed at himself. "She came to me and no
one else is going to get the goodies but me. I have
been waiting for the payoff since I was a teenager."

Chloe's face twisted up and she bit on her finger. When she seemed more composed, she said, "Nell was your first love, wasn't she?"

How do I maintain my manly dignity here? Riley thought. He ran a couple of different scenarios through his head and finally, he popped out, "Yeah, so what?" *That sounded intelligent. That sounded cool.*

She smiled at him. "Boy, you never know about a man and his secrets until you divorce him."

Dee Dee sashayed over to Riley and leaned over so he could get a thorough glimpse of her man-made cleavage. Dee Dee was all about cleavage and swaying hips. "Hi, Riley," she purred. Even Riley had to admit Dee Dee was stacked, with her big boobs, pushed-out butt and narrow waist. She'd added beads to her brown hair that clinked as she turned her head. And while her dark brown complexion was flawlessly made up, she had the overblown look of a rose left too long on the branch.

"I'll have the usual," he said.

"What's that?" She pulled a pencil out of her apron pocket and held out a pad of paper. Her long, scarlet-tipped nails were poised only inches from Riley's face.

Chloe covered her mouth with her hand, trying not to laugh. Her chest started rumbling with voiceless laughter.

"Spanish omelet and coffee."

"Right," Dee Dee replied.

Laughter came from Nell's station and Dee Dee

glanced over at the counter and frowned. "I don't get it. All my regulars have deserted me for Nell."

"Probably because eighteen million trumps your double-Ds anyday," Chloe said.

Ouch, Riley thought. Chloe seemed to be enjoying this way too much.

Dee Dee stared at Chloe as though just remembering she was there. "At least I *am* a double-D." She glanced at Chloe's chest. While Chloe wasn't ample in the chest, she still wore a respectable 36B. Riley knew she kept herself well-toned. Dee Dee should take notes about exercise.

In high school, Dee Dee had always had the guys sniffing after her. Rumors about her sexual prowess had fueled many of the guys' imaginations. Even Riley had flirted a bit with her, but never seriously. He'd been too busy being a bad boy and she'd been too busy being a bad girl. The biggest problem with Dee Dee was that she wasn't a challenge, not like Nell, or even Chloe.

Dee Dee took Chloe's order, though her gaze kept wandering back to her regulars still flirting with Nell. After she flounced off, Chloe dug into Riley again.

"Nell was your first love, wasn't she?"

Riley didn't want to answer her question. How could he explain the connection he'd always had to Nell? "You weren't born in this town."

"What does that have to do with anything?"

"The one thing I wanted was acceptance, but

being from the wrong side of town, with the wrong kind of parents and the wrong attitude made me angry. No matter what, no matter how people told her to stay away from me, Nell never looked at me as though I had some kind of contagious disease. She liked me despite my background." And they'd had something in common. Her parents had abandoned her the same way his had. His father had been an alcoholic who chased women and who had eventually walked away from his family and never came back. His mother had been a long-suffering, Bible-thumping, closet alcoholic who drank in secret and made him macaroni and cheese every night for dinner until he couldn't stand the sight of it. His younger sister had skipped the minute she had the chance to get away. Like him, no one ever expected her to do anything with her life, but she'd fought her way through UCLA and was now a respected lawyer in Los Angeles.

"Oh, you have that look on your face again," Chloe said.

"What the hell look is that?"

"The 'I'm-dealing-with-my-past-bullshit' look," she replied, then took a sip of her coffee.

Yeah, he knew he had himself a trunk load of issues, but his ex wasn't getting it. "Chloe, you're not appreciating how really odd this situation is."

"Am I supposed to?" She leaned forward. "Sometimes I think the whole town of Wayloo is odd, and you're just another aspect of it."

"We came back to be close to your momma and daddy." He snapped his mouth shut because that decision had cost them their son. A look of pain crossed her face and he took her hand. "I'm sorry. Sometimes my mouth just gets away from me."

"I know." She squeezed his hand.

They had a shared memory, too. Even after two years, he could see that Chloe hadn't really dealt with her grief yet and he felt unable to help her, much less himself. Riley, Chloe and Nell had way too many "if only's" from their pasts to deal with.

Dee Dee came back with their breakfast. She placed his Spanish omelet in front of Chloe and her pancakes in front of him. He got Chloe's milk and she got a pot of tea. His coffee seemed to have completely disappeared.

The front door opened and old Buddy McAllister tottered in with his cane tapping away in front of him. He wore an aging tuxedo and held a wilted bouquet of flowers in his hand. His wispy gray hair had been plastered across his bald spot. Riley's mouth fell open. Chloe giggled.

"Nell," Buddy roared to the whole diner. "I've come to marry ya and make an honest woman outta ya."

Nell stopped, her arms outstretched with plates balanced on them. She stared at Buddy. Then she put the plates one by one on the nearest table and put her hands on her hips. "What is wrong with you?"

Buddy tried to get down on one knee, but his cane got in the way. "You gotta marry me."

Nell pursed her lips. "Buddy McAllister, you're too old to be a gigolo. And fix your false teeth." Then she moved around him, turned around and untied her apron from behind her back. "I have had enough. I'm going home." She flung her apron on the floor and stalked out the door.

Riley bolted to his feet and started after her.

"I'll get the check," Chloe said as he pushed past Buddy and out the door after Nell.

"I've had it," Nell yelled as she walked angrily down the street. "I've had it. I've had it. I've had it."

Riley caught up with her and grabbed her arm. "I think you need to get away."

"Do you realize that in the last three days, I've had sixteen marriage proposals. Sixteen. Jasper, Earl, Buddy." She rattled off the rest of the names. "Mind you, none of them ever asked me for a date before they demanded I marry them. I was just fat, desperate Nell. Now, I'm fat, desperate Nell with millions."

"You're not fat. You're not desperate. They are." He ushered her toward his car. "You need to get away. How about a picnic? We could go to the old swimming hole, and since school just started, no one will be there."

Her face brightened. She smiled up at him and Riley felt his heart melt into a puddle. "I'll take you home to change and we'll stop at the market for supplies and we'll make a day of it."

Chapter 5

Nell walked into the house and slammed the door. She stalked down the hall to the kitchen and stood in the doorway, her hands balled into fists. She was so angry she could hardly talk.

Her mother sat at the kitchen table, a mug of coffee in front of her and a plate of half-eaten eggs set to one side. Lucy looked up from reading the morning paper. "Why are you home so early?" Lucy asked, her eyes wide with surprise. "Are you not feeling well?"

Nell raised her fists in frustration. "All those men at the diner were ogling me, proposing to me. They think I'm so desperate, I'll fall on the ground and say, 'I'll be thrilled to marry you so I'm not lonely, and here, have my money because I'm so grateful.' So I just came home."

Lucy looked amused. "Am I correct in assuming you've decided against marrying any of these men?"

Nell glared at her mother. "That would be a yes."

Lucy's eyebrows rose. "Good. Although I have to say it's not like you to leave the diner in the middle of the morning rush, I'm glad you've come home."

"How do you know who I am," Nell suddenly shouted, frustration boiling over. "You've never been around to see enough of me to know who or what I am."

Lucy's mouth opened and closed for a few seconds. Finally, she folded the paper and stood up. "My heavens, that was very disrespectful. I believe you have found your spine."

Surprised at her own behavior, Nell clamped a hand over her mouth and tried not to gag. What the hell was wrong with her?

Lucy raised her chin and narrowed her eyes. "You enjoyed yelling at me, didn't you?"

Nell had, but wasn't going to admit to it. "That would be wrong." She'd never once talked back to her grandmama, never once told her all the things boiling inside her. *My,* she thought, *that was liberating.* Nell had to stop herself from smiling, she was so proud of herself.

She leaned against the kitchen counter. "Yes, it would be," Lucy said, "but it was still fun."

"You're not mad?"

"No." Lucy shook her head. She turned a page

of her newspaper. "What are you going to do with your morning?"

That was good. "I'm going on a picnic with Riley."

Lucy looked thoughtful. "I always liked Riley. I had no idea he'd turn out so well. I knew he'd never waste his opportunities. He is way too smart to fall into the same rut as his parents. He just needed some small bit of direction."

Was Lucy trying to get on Nell's good side? This was making her nervous. She wished her mother would just ask for some money and stop trying to be her friend. "Why don't you just ask me for money?" Nell said, suddenly feeling brazen. "Stop beating around the bush."

Her mother burst out laughing. "What a hussy you are. Talking back to your mama. Leaving your job in the middle of the day and going out on a picnic with the town bad boy. A person would think you're my daughter." Lucy waved her hand as she left the kitchen. "Have a good time, baby girl."

Nell headed to the stairs to change out of her uniform, wondering what had just happened between them.

She searched through her closet for something appropriate for a picnic. In the far back, she saw a white-and-yellow flash and she dug deep and found a pretty sundress she'd bought a few years ago but had never had the courage to wear.

She stripped off her uniform, tossed it on the bed

and pulled the sundress over her head. The fabric billowed and swirled before it finally settled on her, hugging her curves in a way that almost embarrassed her. But, after a few looks in the mirror, she decided the sundress was perfect. If she was going to be a vamp, she needed to look like a vamp.

She dug out a pair of white sandals and slid them on her feet, then she pulled down a box from the overhead shelf. Her grandmother had given her a big, wide-brimmed floppy hat one year for Easter. The ribbon on it was red and didn't match her sundress. She pulled the ribbon off and searched in her drawer for a silk flower she'd worn on another dress. The silk flower was yellow and she pinned it to the brim and then ran down the stairs, her stomach doing flip-flops.

Was she trying too hard? Yes, she wanted to look pretty, but as bad as that sounded, Riley was a sure thing. *A sure thing?* Nell Evans had herself a sure thing. Oh, how strange a journey life had become.

Downstairs, she looked around for her mother but Lucy was nowhere in sight. Nell went out to the front porch and sat on the swing, fanning herself with the hat while she waited for Riley.

Did she really know what she was doing? No, she didn't, but she didn't care. For the first time in her existence she felt alive. She was going out with Riley and all the sharp-tongued busybodies in town would have enough gossip on her to keep themselves in lunches for a year. Too bad she wasn't going to be around to be the talk of the town.

* * *

Riley pulled into Nell's driveway. She sat on the porch swing. Her hair was braided and wrapped around her head like a crown. She looked queenly and innocent in her white-and-yellow dress. She fanned herself with a hat, small tendrils of hair billowing with each pass of the brim.

That couldn't be as bad as touching. Right. If he kept her hands away from his most important extremities, he'd be all right.

He got out of the car and remote-locked the door. She stood up. The hem of her skirt blew up revealing her long shapely legs.

She smiled at him. "You brought me flowers?"

He liked that he could surprise her. "It's all in the details, my dear."

Nell sighed. "That's real sweet of you, Riley, but I'm a sure thing."

The husky sound of her voice waved over him. God, he loved her voice. "No you're not." He leaned over and kissed her on the cheek, lingering an extra second on the soft skin. Taking a quick breath he inhaled the seductive scent of cotton blossom. She was intoxicating. "And don't let anyone ever think you are."

She tilted her head and stared at him as if pondering her answer. "Okay."

"Now let's go and have ourselves a picnic."

Her big eyes looked so hopeful, he couldn't deny her. "I haven't been to the old watering hole since—

I don't know when. And here it is in the middle of the day when kids used to go at night. It makes me feel so naughty." She slanted him a glance and his whole body tightened. "I'm a bad girl now."

He could feel the sin taking root in her. He led her back to his car and opened the door and watched her get in. She dimpled at him with a saucy smile that made his mouth go dry.

The drive to the swimming hole took less than fifteen minutes. All the while he was aware of Nell sitting next to him, getting herself ready for her next lesson. He pulled under a canopy of trees and parked his car. Nell jumped out and smiled at him. She looked totally delectable in her sundress and her straw hat.

The sun was hidden above the spread of tree branches. A few birds twittered at them. Riley spread an old quilt he'd found in the attic of his house over the patchy grass. The swimming hole was serene and quiet. A slight breeze ruffled the leaves, bringing a hint of the Gulf of Mexico with it.

Riley unpacked the food: fried chicken, mashed potatoes and apple pie, all courtesy of Al Massey, the cook at Granny's Diner. He'd picked up a bottle of wine at the liquor store, a pretty red merlot that sparkled in the wineglass when a stray bit of sun hit against it.

He set plates on the quilt and then served the food and wine. For a while, they ate in a comfortable silence. Nell smiled at him as she delicately picked at the food. She was nervous. She kept nibbling at the fried chicken as though it were her enemy.

When they finally finished eating, Riley repacked the leftover food and dishes. When the quilt was clear, he sat back on his heels and jiggled his eyebrows. "Let get to the fun stuff."

Nell tucked her legs under and pulled her skirt over her knees. She licked her lips. "Shouldn't we go somewhere more private?"

"What's more private than here? We're miles from town and the kids are all in school so no one is going to interrupt us."

"But—"

"I like it here, it makes me feel frisky." Again he jiggled his eyebrows at her shocked expression.

"Do men have favorite spots for…well, you know?"

He had to stop himself from laughing. Her total innocence was so heady. "It's a personal choice."

She shifted her position and pulled her skirt to cover more of her exposed skin. "So what do we do next?"

Looking her directly in the eye, he whispered, "Make out." At least her mother couldn't interrupt them here.

"Any techniques you could share?" Reaching up, she twirled a strand of loose hair around her finger.

As wary as she seemed, she was curious. He liked that. She was being a good sport. "Be yourself."

Nell slapped her hands on her legs. "Being myself means I've remained a virgin to age twenty-five. I think I need a new plan."

Part of him wanted to tell her he'd tried to free her, but she just shut him down. He let it go, because he didn't want to ruin the moment now. Right now he had a yearning to run his hands through her hair. He'd had that fantasy since turning fifteen and figuring out that women's hair was sexy. "Let down your hair for me."

"Riley?" Her lips tilted up at one corner and she arched her eyebrows. Her eyes held a mischievous glint.

"Yes, Nell?"

"How is that going to teach me about kissing?"

"I've never seen your hair down. I've been dying to get my hands in it forever."

"Umm-hmm."

"I like to think of it as…inspiration." Not that he needed a whole hellava lot of inspiration. Just her breathing did it for him every time.

She opened her mouth to reply.

Riley shook his finger and interrupted her. "I'm the teacher," he said, pulling out his trump card.

Nell reached behind her head and unpinned the braid. Slowly she began to loosen her hair.

He wished the canopy wasn't quite so thick so he could see her hair in all of its glory. He knew it smelled good, like flowers. He wondered if her hair would be as soft and thick as it looked. He crooked his finger. "Come here."

Nell moved toward him. "Should I keep my eyes closed or open?"

If he wasn't so determined to get into her panties, he'd be laughing his ass off. "What do you want to do?"

Her lips pursed as she thought. "I think I'll try it with my eyes open."

"The secret of a good kiss is to go with the flow. Don't try and control everything."

"I think I can do that." She leaned forward, her lips puckered.

She looked utterly charming. He shifted and slipped his arm around her waist and pulled her toward him. He forced her back to the ground. When she lay on her back, he lowered his lips to hers. Again he was struck by the utter sweetness of her mouth. He could taste the apples from the pie on her lips and tongue. She moved her lips tentatively. He could feel her heated breath on his face. The soft cotton-blossom scent, laced with a hint of orange, seduced him. His senses went into overdrive. Heat seeped down to his belly and he was hard and heavy from the want of her.

Nell was like a drug in his system, taking over his every waking moment until he could get his next fix. No one had a twelve-step program for her. And he didn't want to recover from her anytime soon. Their lips melted together. Her lips were soft and pliant against his. Her body pressed into his as if she was made to fit him.

Riley's hands roamed over Nell's lush curves. After all the fantasies and daydreams he'd had about her, nothing compared to touching the real thing.

The feel of her body couldn't be paralleled. A woman's voluptuous body was always territory to be discovered and conquered, but no woman compared to the mystery of Nell. Even through her clothes she enticed him. He couldn't begin to envision what touching her flesh would be like when there were no barriers between them, skin to skin, naked.

She had a womanly softness he'd never experienced before. His head told him it couldn't just be her curves. There had to be more. He could spend the rest of his life trying to figure it out. He'd be more than willing to.

It was just Nell, plain and simple.

She had him in her spell, he'd never begin to understand.

A smart man would just give up and go with the flow or get the hell out right now. But he needed to know why she'd held him captive for so long.

He slid his mouth over her cheek and down to the curve of her neck. He ran his tongue over the beating pulse. He swore he could almost hear the blood singing in her veins. Without thinking, he slipped his hand under her skirt and touched the bare skin of her thigh.

He just knew any moment she would pull away and tell him to stop, but she didn't. Instead, she arched her body closer to his. He was going to explode from the need.

His other hand glided under her skirt to her stomach. She was all softness and silk. Not like a woman who did two hundred crunches to obtain muscles. No, she was womanly and smooth. He felt her skin contract under his fingers.

He kept waiting for her to pull back, but she didn't. Silently he thanked God she didn't. It was as if she were giving him permission to explore to his heart's content. He wasn't the type of man to turn down such a seductive invitation. Her hands seemed to be doing some investigating of their own. He liked how she was bold enough to touch him.

His lips moved back up to hers and their tongues danced. She picked up the fine art of kissing with little instruction from him.

Shifting his body he settled himself in between her legs. She was already wet for him. The knowledge speeding to his head pushed him over the edge. He wanted her so bad he thought he was going to die. He massaged her thigh, letting his fingers travel up until he encountered cotton. He slipped his hand over her hips. Her panties didn't seem to end. The last time he'd touched cotton briefs was a long-ago memory. Granny panties he'd heard them called. Somehow they didn't seem right for Nell anymore.

Carefully he slipped his fingers under the elastic of her panties. Immediately he felt her damp heat. Soft curls wrapped around his fingers. She was so wet for him. He thought he was going to burst. The blood rushed out of his head and headed down to his raging hard-on. He could feel his stomach contract. If she could make him any hotter, he'd burn up.

Dare he go further? They were only supposed to

kiss. He had gone beyond simple into the extreme. He kept waiting for her to stop him, but nothing happened. In fact, her mouth became more demanding.

Okay, he thought, she was into it. He gently inserted a finger inside her. Hot wetness surrounded him. Her muscles clenched around him instantly. Her body stiffened.

Her legs clenched harder around him and she pulled her mouth off his.

Riley tried to withdraw his finger, but his hand was trapped between her legs.

"What are you doing down there?" Her voice was breathless and shocked.

What did a guy say at a moment like this. *Oh, just checking your oil.* "I can't move my hand."

Her legs still didn't loosen up. "I wasn't expecting you to do that."

"I got ahead of myself." His hand was going numb. "But if you unglue your legs—"

"It feels so nice."

Nice? Now that really hurt a guy's ego. "Then why are you ready to snap me in half with your legs?"

"I'm just a little startled. I didn't expect it to feel so good."

"You don't want me to stop?"

She shook her head. "Well, no."

Sweet. He knew how far he wanted to go. At least as far as they'd gone the other night. Only it was his turn to do her. "How far do you think you want to go?"

Nell bit her bottom lip. "I know I don't want you to stop, but I'm not sure how far I want you to go at this juncture."

He had to laugh. This conversation sounded as if they were on some sort of road trip. "What am I going to do with you, Nell?"

She smiled, but didn't say anything.

"Would you like me to show you how you can feel really good?"

"Yes. Please."

"If I do anything you don't like just let me know without snapping my fingers off. Promise?"

She smiled and nodded her head as if she were a trusting child. "I promise."

"Lie back, relax and loosen your legs."

She complied.

Riley began to gently stroke inside her. With each caress he felt her body relax against his. Her honey began to flow. She squirmed underneath him. Her back arched. And he heard a sigh escape her lips. He could feel her nipples, hardened against his chest.

He found her clit, slick and hard. He began rubbing her flesh in a slow circle with the pad of his thumb. He used his other finger to delve into her hot depths. He wanted to kiss her, but he found he enjoyed watching her face react to each of the new sensations.

The sunlight caught the creamy brown of her skin. He could make out a faint flush of pleasure on her cheeks. Her mouth opened and her tongue licked her bottom lip. He had never seen a woman so beautiful before. He'd wanted to do just this for such a long time. Part of him had a hard time believing this wasn't just one of his random fantasies.

"Riley, oh, Riley."

"Just go with it, baby. Just let yourself go." He circled her moistness, one finger deep inside, the other on her most tender spot, massaging until she squirmed.

She fisted the shoulders of his shirt. Her long legs wrapped around his hips. "Riley. I feel…I feel…like I'm…" she took a deep breath as if to control herself "…I'm going to die."

He increased the speed of his caress—in and out, slow and fast. He wanted to push her over the edge and feel her come in his arms. He'd never wanted to give a woman pleasure so badly before. Her body began to tremble and Nell buried her face in his neck. She tensed in his arms. Her teeth sank into his flesh. Her inner muscles gripped his finger and her body began to shake. He heard her call out his name.

Oh yeah. He'd made her come for the very first time. It wasn't triumph he felt. Something he couldn't name. Something that made him very nervous.

Nell walked up the front steps feeling a little disappointed. She'd had greater expectations for her afternoon at the swimming hole, but a bunch of kids ditching school had sabotaged that idea.

The sun was low on the horizon. She had grass

stains on her dress and her hair was mussed. But she felt good. Naughty. A glow radiated through her that made her feel as though she were sitting on top of the world.

She pushed open the screen door and walked past the living room and down the hall to the kitchen. Her mother sat in the kitchen, her bare feet resting in a large plastic tub of steaming water.

"Mama, why are you soaking your feet?" On closer inspection, she realized her mother was wearing one of the diner uniforms.

"I had a hard day at the diner." Lucy opened her eyes and turned her head toward Nell.

"I realize you're wearing your old uniform, but what were you doing at the diner?"

"I worked your shift. And then Juanita called in sick so I stayed to work the dinner rush." She reached into her pocket and pulled out a thick roll of money. "I made me a hundred and fifty dollars in tips. Not as good as when I worked the Battle Scarred Bar, but damn good."

Nell couldn't believe what she was hearing. "You worked my shift?"

Lucy glanced up. "I know how to work. I was slinging hash and making coffee at the diner before you were born, baby girl. Now you go on and have yourself a nice shower, you have grass in your hair."

"You and I are gonna be having a long talk in our future." Nell reached up and pulled a piece of foliage out of her hastily fashioned braid.

"That's why I'm here," Lucy said and raised one foot and started to massage it.

Nell dropped the piece of grass into the trash container and turned on her heel, walking down the hall to the stairs and up to her room.

She didn't know what to think about her mama, but she had a lot to think about Riley.

After her shower, she sat down at her desk and pulled out her notebook. Rapidly, she wrote down all that had happened and how she'd felt. Remembering her first orgasm was almost painful. How could she have lived so many years and not known how a man could pleasure a woman?

When she finished her notes, she turned on her computer. When she hooked into the Internet, she went to her mailbox. She had two e-mails. One was from the real estate agent looking for a condo for her in New York. She'd thought about staying in the dorm when she went to college, but she knew that would never do for her.

She wasn't a giggly eighteen-year-old anymore. In fact, she never had been a giggly eighteen-year-old. The man suggested she come to New York and go around with him and he also embedded several Web addresses for her to take virtual tours. But when she read the purchase price of each piece of property, she almost had a stroke.

Who knew real estate in New York was so expensive? Her grandmother had always told her to buy real estate, but a two-bedroom apartment costing three million dollars was way too expensive for her. She had to make her money last for the rest of her life.

She didn't want to fritter away her inheritance. A part of her wanted to buy all the things she'd wanted all her life, like sheets that cost five thousand dollars, but another part of her wanted to sit on the money until it multiplied. She was torn between wanting to spend something, and not spending a penny. Deep down inside, she figured she had a lot more of her grandmother in her than she'd ever suspected. She didn't want to be eighty years old, alone and broke— nor did she want to hoard every penny and begrudge herself the most basic items the way her grandmother had.

Wasting the money on fripperies seemed disrespectful to her grandmother who had worked hard. She couldn't be angry with her grandmother for the way she'd saved and pinched her pennies. Because her grandfather had run away with the town floozy, her grandmother had had to make do on her own.

Nell's mind went back and forth over the money. Finally, she covered her face with her hands. She didn't know who she was or what she really wanted. She did know she wanted to go to New York City and attend school, but after that her future stretched out in an aimless wandering. She didn't even know yet what she wanted to major in.

With a half sigh, she opened the second e-mail. NYU had answered her query about an interview for admission in the spring. A woman had written back suggesting she make a quick visit to the campus and selected a date three weeks away. Nell could make that appointment. Fly in and fly out in two days. She shivered with excitement. Now she just had to wait for answers from Columbia and Fordham.

Finally, she was moving forward in her life. Toward what end, she didn't know. But she was going to do something more with her life than live in a small town and be the object of gossip.

Riley couldn't sleep. He tossed and turned for hours, going over his day with Nell and all that had happened. At 3:00 a.m., he finally got out of bed. He stood at the open window and looked out over the street. His house was set back from the street and his nearest neighbor was half a block away.

He couldn't stay still. Finally, he pulled on jeans and a T-shirt and went down to his workshop. Maybe if his hands were occupied, he would stop thinking.

In the garage he opened the door and then pulled his toolbox toward his old motorcycle. The Harley had belonged to his dad and was the only thing he had of his father's. By the time his dad had abandoned the family, the bike no longer worked. Riley had made it his responsibility to bring the old piece back to life. Part of him needed to fix something and make it right. He could do that with the motorcycle.

He sat cross-legged on the concrete and stared at the Harley. The only good memories of his father were entwined with the old bike. Riley had taken the bike to school in Chicago, and when he'd sold it to get a down payment for an apartment for him, Chloe and the coming baby, they'd had their first fight. She'd worked double shifts for nearly a month to buy it back. And when Benjy was strong enough to sit up, they'd sit for hours on the bike together. Benjy had liked sitting on the seat and pretending to ride. He'd made motor noises and growls and pretended to steer. Riley had been so excited to be able to pass the bike on to his son. "Rorocycle" was one of the first words his son had said that he could really understand.

Tears pricked the back of Riley's eyes. Benjy had been the love of his life. Chester woke and seemed to understand Riley's sad mood; the dog moved close to Riley and lay down next to his knee. Riley had been talking to Chester for a long time.

Riley slid his fingers down the back of the dog's silky head. "Sorry, old boy, you must have been chasing rabbits or Miss Gracie's Pomeranian. That would never have worked out with you two." He scratched Chester's head.

Chester whined and rested his head on Riley's lap.

"I intended to restore the Harley for Benjy. I wanted him to have good memories about it." Riley had wanted to reclaim the motorcycle to get rid of the bad memories he had of his father. Riley's father used to ride off with his cycle buddies to go drinking and carousing at the tavern, and Riley had always wanted to get on the back of the motorcycle and go with his father.

The little boy inside him always figured if he could prove to his dad what a good son he was, maybe his dad would stay home and not drink. And they would do the father-son things other fathers and sons did. But finally, he'd given up and gone his own way. If he couldn't get his father's praise, he'd settle for the town of Wayloo's scorn.

Riley had been an adult before he realized he would never have those things with his own father no matter how desperately he wanted them, so he'd started building those memories with Benjy, only to have Benjy taken away.

Benjy's death was Riley's punishment for his own mistakes. He'd been arrogant to think he could out-father his own dad. He'd wanted to prove he was a better father, and that would have been his revenge. How stupid he was to think such thoughts.

Chapter 6

The next morning, Nell woke bright and early to the sun streaming into her bedroom, highlighting the practical neutral palette her grandmother and she had chosen. Why was there so much beige and brown in her room? She sat up and looked around at the heavy wood furniture, the old brown carpet and the plain beige walls. Drab. Drab. Drab.

She could repaint. She lay in bed, arms behind her head, staring at the ceiling. She had the option, what color would she choose? She ran colors through her mind and tried to see her bedroom in each of them. Rust? No. Red? No. Green? No. Damn! That wasn't a color.

Finally, she rolled out of bed, showered and

dressed in her work uniform, dreading going to work. When she went downstairs, she found her mother sitting at the kitchen table sipping her morning coffee and reading the newspaper. Like Nell, Lucy was dressed in the diner uniform.

"Mama," Nell said, "what are you doing?" Lucy couldn't be going to the diner to work again. She had never demonstrated such determination before. Lucy had always been someone who'd flitted from job to job, man to man, day to day.

"Reading the newspaper, baby girl," Lucy said as she turned a page of the newspaper.

"But you're wearing the diner uniform?"

"I'm going to work your shift." Lucy waved her hand in the air. "You shouldn't have to face all those old men slobbering over you."

"Are you trying to get on my good side?" Nell didn't like feeling so cynical, but in the past, her mama never did anything unless she was getting something out of her good deed.

Lucy grinned. "Yes, I am."

Something died in Nell at that moment. Somehow she'd found herself hoping for more. Hoping for something she could believe in.

Lucy smiled. "But not for the reasons you think." She stood, picked up her coffee mug and drained it. She checked her watch, said, "I'm going to be late," and rinsed her mug and placed it on the drain board. Then she walked out the back door and left Nell with her mouth open.

What did Lucy mean? Nell poured herself coffee and sat down at the table. Here she was ready to go to work, and now she didn't have to. She felt odd, as though something had been lost.

The sound of a car drew her to the window to see a battered truck pull into the driveway. She watched as Steely McNeal stepped out and walked over to the back door. She hoped he'd put his dentures in now that he was finally getting around to proposing.

Steely knocked politely and when Nell opened the door, she found him standing on the back stoop dressed in frayed overalls, a straw hat neatly on his head and his dark brown eyes contemplating her sadly.

Steely McNeal had never married, and, even though he was only in his early forties, gossip in town said he just wasn't the marrying kind.

"Mr. McNeal," she said, stiffening as she waited for the marriage proposal sure to follow—though he didn't have flowers. "Can I help you?"

"Can I come in, Miz Nell?" His polite tone set her guard up even more. Thank God, he'd put his teeth in.

Nell stood aside to let him into the kitchen. As he entered, he tore his hat from his head. She'd known Steely most of her life. She'd gone to school with his much younger sister who currently worked at the post office. He owned a modest farm five miles up the road that had been handed down in his family for the last hundred and twenty years. He was one of the last independent farmers in the area.

"I just stopped by," he said, "to tell you how sorry I was to hear about your grandmama's passing. She was a generous woman."

"My grandmother?" Nell poured him a mug of coffee and held it out to him. "Would you like to sit down?" Relief flooded her—he hadn't come to propose.

He accepted the cup of coffee, but not the invitation to sit. "Your grandma was a crusty old girl. Don't get me wrong. She was a stickler for manners and punctuality. She liked what she liked and no one could tell her different, but if you needed something, your grandmama was the first one to offer help. I don't want to mention Hurricane Katrina, but your grandmama loaned a lot of us money to help rebuild. If not for her, we'd still be waiting for all the federal money. None of us had to come to her, she came to us and told us whatever we needed, she'd be proud to help."

Nell leaned against the counter, staring at the man. Her grandmother did all that? How come Nell hadn't known?

Steely held his hat in his hand looking awkward. Nell felt sorry for him. "I didn't know that about my grandmother."

"Miz Sarah, she was right tight with a nickel, but she helped me out when my crops failed last year. She gave me a loan, enough to tide me over until my next harvest. I just wanted you to know, I'll pay you back in full then."

Nell realized she hadn't really dealt with her grandmother's business affairs. She needed to check with the accountant, Mr. Groves, to find out what else she needed to know. "I know you'll make good on your loan, Mr. McNeal." Nell didn't know what else to say to the man; he was so obviously uncomfortable and she didn't want him to think she was being rude. Who else owed her grandmother money?

"Thank you, Miz Nell. I gotta get back to the farm." He opened the back door and stepped out, plopped his hat on his head and stepped lively out to his truck to drive off in a hail of dust.

Nell felt so confused. Her grandmother had been gone for three weeks and Nell was just starting to realize she had never really known the woman at all. How could her grandmama be so generous with so many people and so stingy with Nell, her blood kin?

She went to her room and changed into jeans, a T-shirt and sneakers. She needed to talk to someone and the only person she could think of was Riley.

Riley stood on the sidewalk, camera in hand, eyes trained on the old Thompson house. Old Mr. Thompson had died two years ago and his son had inherited the house. Charley Thompson wanted to restore the old house to its nineteenth-century glory. But the task was going to be a tough one. Wood rot had settled into the foundation as well as termites. The inside had been chopped up into little rooms old Mr. Thompson had rented out to supplement his Social Security.

Despite all the changes made on the house, it was still beautiful, with original plaster moldings and a hand-carved cypress fireplace mantel. Once it was restored, Riley knew the house would be beautiful.

Riley snapped photos of the house from every angle. When he looked up from his contemplation, he saw Nell walking down the street toward him, purpose in every step.

"Riley," Nell said as she approached, "I need to talk to you."

His stomach clenched. With their picnic yesterday—and the feel of her body—still fresh in his mind, he could think of nothing better than a can of whipped cream and a quiet place to "talk." Well, talk wasn't what he had in mind. They still had one more step.

"Nell, I'd be happy to talk."

"Riley," Nell said sharply, "stop looking like that."

"Like what?" he asked, hoping he appeared a hundred times more innocent then he felt.

"Like you're going to eat me."

Now she was getting with the program. "I am not going there. Not right now and not in public." Most definitely not in public.

She covered her cheeks with her hands and looked at him in confusion. Riley loved the way she looked when she didn't know what to say.

She shaded her eyes with her hand. "Riley, did you know my grandmother lent Steely McNeal money? Did you know she gave people money to help rebuild after Katrina?"

This wasn't what he'd hoped she'd want to talk about. "Are you upset because she loaned people money?"

Nell glared at him. "I'm not upset the way you think I'm upset." She rubbed her eyes. She'd been crying. "I just wish I had known all these things before she died."

"Come on," he said taking her by the arm, "you need to sit down." He led her up the cracked sidewalk to the wraparound veranda.

"I'm mad," she said when he settled her down on the top step, "because I didn't know that part of her and didn't always have nice thoughts about her. She was this whole other person I didn't even know. Who else did she loan money to? Or help?"

"Well," Riley said, "she helped me."

She gave him a sharp glance. "You! She didn't even like you."

"I know she didn't like me, and she wasn't my favorite person either. But, a little-known fact around Wayloo High School was that I was a pretty good student. I may have worn a leather jacket, ridden a motorcycle and acted like a juvenile delinquent, but I was smart. I even made it on the honor roll."

She pointed to her chest. "I never saw your name."

"Principal Callahan was willing to keep me off. Being smart is one thing, but having people know you're smart takes away cool points."

"Aren't the people in my life full of surprises?"

Nell mused in a wry tone. "Makes me wonder what else I don't know about my grandmother."

"Are you angry?"

Nell gave him a long level look. "She offered to help you, but never once offered to help me. I know she was afraid of being alone, but she always made me feel that if I took one step out of this town, I'd never come back and she would die of loneliness."

He could understand that. He forced himself not to think about what would happen after Nell left for her big adventure in New York. "Are you planning on coming back from New York?"

She tapped her chin. "I don't know. I just want a new life. I'm tired of being boring good girl Nell Evans who wears cotton underwear."

"But I like boring good girl Nell Evans. Always have." Riley understood Nell's grandma in a way he didn't think Nell ever would. He tried to explain anyway. "Your grandmother lost a lot of people who were really important to her. I think the thought of losing you was too much for her. Especially after she became ill."

"She never gave me a chance." A tear ran down Nell's cheek.

He wanted to comfort her, but wasn't certain how. "You're right, and what she did was wrong, but she still loved you." Riley knew Miz Sarah had always loved Nell.

Nell wiped the tear off her cheek. "Come on," she said, standing up and tugging on his hand.

"Where are we going?"

"We're gonna walk to the cemetery while I still have this righteous indignation and can yell at my grandmother. Then I'm going to move on with my life." She stalked down the sidewalk to the street and turned toward the high, white steeple of the church and the cemetery beyond.

Riley didn't want to follow, but he did, mostly out of curiosity; he wanted to know what Nell was going to say to a dead woman.

The cemetery was cool and serene with towering live oaks and a few poplars. The area nearest the gate held graves going back two hundred years. Most of the memorials were scattered with no particular order to them, but beyond the gate where the newer interments were, the graves tended to be in more orderly rows.

Nell walked down the long rows to her grandmother's grave. Even though no headstone yet adorned the place, Nell moved unerringly to the spot marked only by a slight disturbance and a depression in the ground.

She stood to the side of the depression and glared at the ground. Finally, she sat down and covered her face with her hands.

"Nell," Riley said, "do you want me to leave so you can have your conversation alone?"

Nell peeked through her fingers. "I'm already having that conversation—in my head."

"Okay, if you say so."

She shrugged. "I can yell at my grandmother in my head, but not out loud."

He couldn't help the chuckle that escaped. Nell was precious. He couldn't think of any other person in his life who would walk a mile to yell at her grandmother's grave and then do it in her head.

"Why not do it out loud?"

"I don't want anyone to hear me."

"We're alone."

Her hands dropped from her face. "Yelling in a cemetery seems disrespectful."

Riley had a lot to answer for in his own past. One thing he'd done, and told no one about, was have sex with Mary-Lee Ashforth in the cemetery. He looked around and spied the old oak and remembered that night. Mary-Lee had been awesome.

He leaned against a headstone and waited. He wondered what Nell was saying to her grandmother and wondered if he should ask.

Suddenly, Nell took a deep breath and stood up. "Okay, I'm done. Let's go buy a car today."

"A car?"

"Yes. I want…I want…I want that cute blue Mini Cooper on Jennie Washington's car lot."

Riley was amazed. She could have any car in the whole world and she wanted a used Mini Cooper. "What do you need a car for? You can use your grandmother's car." Well maybe not, the old beige Buick was over twenty years old and probably didn't have more than a hundred miles on it.

She grimaced. "I hate that car. It's like driving an aircraft carrier. It's an old-lady car. I want something young and fun. Like my life is going to be." Her tone was wistful.

At least the Mini Cooper was small. She couldn't get into a lot of trouble. Unless she decided to go one-on-one with a Mack truck.

"That Mini Cooper used to be Laurie Taylor's and she had a race car engine put in it. I can't wait to get behind the wheel." Nell clapped her hands in delight. "I'm gonna go zipping around all the back roads just like I wanted to do when I was in high school."

Good Lord, she was going to kill herself. "Are you planning on reliving your teenage years?" he asked, his heart in his throat at the thought of her zipping around and terrorizing the local population.

"I have no desire to be sixteen again. But I love the look of the Mini Cooper. It's small and cute and—"

He didn't know why, but he felt the need to stop her. "What are you going to do with a car in New York City? No one has a car there."

She rested one hand on her hip and gazed at him. "Then I'll have the streets all to myself."

Riley groaned. He was unleashing a monster on the world. He didn't think Wayloo was ready for her version of *The Fast and the Furious*. Hell, he didn't think Wayloo was ready for the new Nell.

"You've seen me drive," Nell said. "What are you worried about?"

"If you drive your grandmother's car, you'll be safer. All that reinforced steel between you and the telephone poles would make me feel better."

She put her hands on her hips and glared at him. "You have a motorcycle. Or as Doc Jones likes to call them, a donor cycle."

"But I know what I'm doing." And his reckless days were behind him. Maturity, marriage and fatherhood did that to a guy.

"Why?" She tilted her head at him, her eyes narrowing. "Because you're a man and men get to live in the fast lane while I have to drive some old Buick because it's safe and I'm a woman? I don't think so."

How did he make her understand that cars weren't the safest thing in the world. Hurtling down the street at fifty miles per hour—a sudden stop did things to a person's body. And mix that with alcohol… His thoughts skittered away from his son's death. "You're not the only one in this relationship. I can worry about you if I want."

"We don't have a relationship beyond friendship," she retorted. "And maybe sex."

Since they hadn't gotten to the sex part, yet, he wasn't sure they even had that. "And friends don't let friends buy unsafe little cars and speed down some back road. And why are you buying a used car anyway? You can afford a new one. You're rich." Hell, she was filthy rich, but it seemed Nell was more like her grandmother than she thought.

She slanted a glance at him. "I want to stay rich.

I read this article on lottery winners. No matter how much wealth they won, ninety percent of them were bankrupt within ten years. I'm not going to be bankrupt. My grandmother sacrificed a lot to make sure she wouldn't have to rely on anyone. And I'm not going to waste her money."

She had started back toward the gates when she stopped, her eyes drawn to something. She picked her way through the headstones. Riley followed her, wondering what had caught her attention. And when she stopped, he knew.

She stood in front of Benjy's grave. "How come there's no headstone on Benjy's grave?" she asked, turning to face him, condemnation in her eyes.

Riley stiffened. He started to shake, his gut clenched up and sweat popped out on his forehead. He turned on his heel and walked away. He needed to get away. Anyplace would do, as long as he was as far from his son's grave as he could get. He stumbled over a marker and went down on his knees. He couldn't breathe.

Nell reached to help him up. "Riley. Riley, are you all right?"

He pressed a hand against his chest, the tightness a thick steel band around him as though he were about to have a heart attack. He couldn't breathe. He couldn't think. "Go away, Nell."

"But, Riley." She placed a hand on his shoulder. "What's wrong?"

Tears gathered in his eyes and he wiped them

away impatiently. "Don't, Nell. Don't touch me." He glanced up. "Go away. Leave me the hell alone."

"But, Riley, I want to help you."

"Go away."

Nell backed away, her face filled with sadness and sympathy. She nodded, then turned and left, walking down the path that lead to the entrance to the cemetery.

Riley sat on the ground, holding his pain to himself. He couldn't look at Benjy's grave. He couldn't even think about Benjy. He rolled out flat and lay looking up at the blue sky and white billowing clouds.

Life wasn't fair, he thought through the darkness of his pain. Life was never fair.

Nell ran out of the cemetery trying not to look back. She didn't want to intrude on Riley's pain. She'd had no idea Riley still felt so deeply over his son's death. Benjy had been gone for almost two years. She understood his grief, but he seemed mired in it, unable to move beyond it.

She stood in front of the church trying to decide what to do. Then she started walking. The only person who came to mind was Chloe.

She walked down Main Street eyeing the buildings. Wayloo had been growing the last ten years. The original two-block-long main street had become four. Antique stores had drawn a small but growing tourist trade. The hair salon had expanded into the empty store next door. Several bed-and-breakfasts had opened in older houses that had been restored. Chloe's house was the best of them. Riley had restored the house to it's pre-World War I glory after they had divorced.

Chloe's house was a solid three-story Craftsman-style house with lots of wood and a porch supported by thick pillars. Nell marched up the front sidewalk to the veranda, opened the door and walked inside.

Chloe was in the dining room clearing a table. She looked up at Nell and smiled. "Nell. How is the Wayloo version of the cele-butante?"

"I'm fine." Nell's voice cracked as she gave Chloe a slight smile and suddenly burst into tears.

Chloe set the plates down on the table, went to Nell and drew her out of the dining room into a small office set off to the side of the entry. She settled Nell on a chair.

"What's wrong, Nell?" Chloe asked, gently putting her hand on Nell's arm.

"Riley."

"What did Riley do to you?" Chloe demanded.

Nell couldn't catch her breath to answer. The image of Benjy's grave, unadorned by any memorial, sent her off into fresh tears. How could one little boy be so ignored?

"I'll kill him," Chloe said, beating a tattoo on the desk. "I told him this was a bad idea. You're a nice woman and you deserve better then to be humped and dumped."

While Chloe ranted on and on, Nell's tears increased. She sobbed and gulped. After some time, she took several calming breaths and forced herself to stop crying. She wiped tears from her eyes and when she could finally talk again, she took Chloe's hand and squeezed it tightly. "Chloe, it's all my fault," she wailed. "I didn't know."

Chloe pulled up a chair and sat next to Nell. She took hold of her hand and squeezed it tight. "Calm down, sweetie. Take a few nice, deep breaths and let them out very slowly. Now tell me what happened."

Nell did as instructed and found herself calming down enough to get the words out. "I went to the cemetery to yell at my grandmother."

"She passed." Chloe raised an eyebrow. "What did yelling at her accomplish?"

Nell swallowed and took a deep breath. "For starters, I felt better. I was angry over the money."

"Did Riley go with you?"

"Yes," Nell replied. "And afterward, we started talking about me getting a Mini Cooper with a race-car engine and he said he didn't think it was safe and…and…I was leaving when I thought he might want to visit with Benjy and when I got there, I realized Benjy's grave didn't have a headstone and when I asked him why not, then he just…he just…" Her voice trailed off.

"He had himself an emotional meltdown," Chloe said.

Nell stopped crying. She wiped away the tears that tracked down her face. "How do you know?"

Chloe sighed. "Riley refuses to deal with Benjy's passing. That's why he doesn't have a headstone. Riley can't pick one out and I hate to push him. He feels responsible because he should have taken better care of our son."

"He was killed by a drunk driver. How is that anyone's fault but the man who killed him?"

Chloe shook her head. "A lot goes back to his own childhood and his parents' problems. I'll be honest, Nell. Riley married me because I got pregnant, not because I was the love of his life. He married me because that is what a noble, honorable man does. He took his responsibilities seriously. You should have seen him the day Benjy was born. He held Benjy in his arms and promised him he would never be like his father. He would never abandon him. When Benjy passed, something stopped in Riley. And I guess he figures if he acknowledges his pain, he might forget."

Nell nibbled at her thumb a moment. "How am I going to fix that?"

"Other than time, I don't know," Chloe said with a sigh. "I've already tried."

"How do *you* deal with the pain?"

A tear slipped down Chloe's cheek. "I just keep moving forward. It's all I know to do."

Nell suspected Chloe was just putting on a great big smiley face to mask her pain. Chloe was the busiest woman in three states. She was building an empire in Wayloo. She owned a bookstore and the bed-and-breakfast, and she was the coowner of the beauty salon and the best bakery in five states. Chloe wasn't anywhere near over her child's death. She just kept herself too busy to deal with it.

"And you keep taking care of Riley," Nell said, her own sorrow for her grandmother giving her a rare understanding into Chloe. "Why?"

Chloe said, "I have my reasons."

Nell didn't understand and wanted to go deeper. For some strange reason, she wanted to know what made Riley tick. He was fun, handsome and charming. But today was the first time she'd seen depth to Riley. Up until now, he'd always been Mr. Good Time. Even after Benjy's death, he'd never shown as much emotion as he'd shown today.

"Are you sure you're not still in love with him?" Nell asked.

Chloe smiled. "I'm always going to love him, and I'll never regret marrying him, but I don't have the love for him a woman should have for a man she marries."

Nell frowned, trying to interpret Chloe's comment. "That is very complicated."

"That's how I feel, too." Chloe gave a little laugh. "Why did you ask me if I was still in love with him?"

Nell blurted out, "Because you're my friend."

"That was one rush of an answer. Now tell me the truth."

Nell looked away. "I don't know. I just know Riley has always been special to me." More than special. He'd provided her with an anchor she hadn't even known she needed.

"Nell, you don't have to go to New York City."

Nell bit her lip. "I don't know what you mean by that."

Chloe gave her a sharp, penetrating look. "Yes, you do."

"Regardless, New York is my dream and I'm going no matter what."

Chloe stood and brushed off her skirt. "We'll see. Now, I have to think about dinner for my guests."

Nell gave Chloe a little kiss on the cheek and walked out the front door into the hot afternoon sun. "Don't forget you're shopping with me on Saturday."

Chloe smiled. "I'm going to make sure you shop until the car is filled with clothes."

Nell smiled, happy to see a smile return to her friend's face. "Now if that isn't a fantasy come true."

Chapter 7

Riley roared down the dirt road, the power of his motorcycle a vibration between his thighs. Plumes of dust floated up on both sides of him, nearly choking him, but he didn't care. Maybe if he went fast enough, he could outrace his pain. The wheel hit a bump and he went airborne for a second before settling back on the road.

He was embarrassed at his breakdown at the cemetery and that Nell had witnessed him coming unglued. He'd thought he had everything under control. Two years should have been enough time to heal, enough time to put his life back into some kind of order, yet there he was crying like a baby in front of her.

He slowed as he came to a junction in the road. To one side, water moved sluggishly through the cypress trees. On the other side was dense forest. When he saw the road was clear, he accelerated through the junction. If he drove himself hard enough, he would just forget and maybe he would stop aching. More than anything else in the world, he wanted to stop the pain from eating at him. ·

He wanted to forget the last two years. He'd searched for solace and couldn't find it in the bottom of a bottle, in the bedroom of a woman or in one of his wild rides through the bayous. Only when he was with Nell did Benjy's death cease to hover about him, beating him down.

Nell chased the shadows away with her sweet innocence. That was why he ate at the diner every day. He wanted her light to shine on him. Until this moment he hadn't figured that out. But the last few days, after spending more time with her, he found himself pushing the pain a little deeper inside.

The roar of the Harley reverberated through the trees. Sometimes, he thought, if he moved fast enough, he'd outrun all the demons, but not even blinding speed had the power to keep his grief at bay.

But what would he be without the pain? The pain drove him, consumed him, kept him moving through the empty days and nights. He didn't know if he could breath without it. Hell, he was afraid even to try.

He accelerated more, the trees flying past him in

a blur. Eighty miles an hour. Ninety miles an hour. One little twist of the handlebars and he would soar into space. Maybe all the way to heaven and Benjy.

He hit a bump, the motorcycle wobbled. He slowed, realizing maybe he wasn't ready for death yet.

He came to a clearing and braked to a stop. A family of deer browsed in the center of the clearing. The mothers with their almost-grown children raised their heads, startled into worry. But he stopped, turned off the cycle and peace descended on the clearing.

He got off the bike and stood in the shadows watching the deer, wondering why they weren't rushing off. Though the mothers moved to stand between him and their children, they didn't appear too worried.

He sat down on the ground and continued his vigil.

His pain was a part of him now as much as his skin. Nothing would bring Benjy back. He remembered the way Benjy had felt in his arms only moments after his birth. His tiny face had been all scrunched up. And in that moment, Riley's life had been absolutely perfect. His past, who he was and where he had come from, had stopped mattering to him. Benjy's birth had scrubbed away all the past dirt and created a clean slate for Riley. And he'd made a promise to Benjy that he would be the best man, the best father he could possibly be.

But he'd failed. His son was dead and his life was going nowhere.

* * *

Nell opened the door to the diner and stepped into the cool interior. The booths were mostly full, the lunch rush was over and everyone was finishing up their meals. Dee Dee flounced around her station like a little queen bee. Lucy stood behind the snack bar, leaning forward and flirting with Sheriff Atkins. As she talked to the sheriff, she filled up her salt and pepper containers.

Sheriff Atkins was a big, burly man. He had a broad face, dark brown eyes and skin the color of dark cocoa. He'd just survived a nasty divorce from a wife who had run off with another man. Nell knew he was on the rebound, and she worried her mother would be taking advantage of him. He was a nice man and a good tipper. Too nice for her mother. She was going to nip this in the bud. She was used to having her mother upset her life, but for Lucy to set her sights on Sheriff Atkins was a whole other story.

Lucy finished filling the salt and pepper shakers and leaned her elbows on the counter listening to Sheriff Atkins, a playful expression on her face. Nell tried not to frown. She knew her mother was here because she wanted something and wherever her mother went, chaos seemed to follow.

Nell sat down next to Sheriff Atkins. "Good morning, Sheriff. How are you doing?"

He swivelled on the stool. "Mornin', Miss Nell." He gave her a friendly nod. "Your mama here has been telling me all about the Bahamas and her trip there. I'd like to go someday. Lay on the beach and think about nothing, except when my next meal is coming."

Lucy laughed. "Sure, your idea of a vacation is two weeks at your mountain cabin in West Virginia fishing, where you don't have to shave or bathe, or let anyone else touch the remote control."

He grinned at her, having the good grace to look a little embarrassed. "You know a man needs a little change every now and again."

Yeah, right, Nell thought. He didn't need to make a change with her mother. She'd eat him for breakfast and spit out the bones for the rats. "I understand. I'm looking for a change, myself."

Lucy tapped the counter. "Yep, my baby is moving to the big city all by herself."

The pride in her mother's voice surprised her. Nell wondered why Lucy felt that way. Nell's decision had nothing to do with her mother and everything to do with her own needs.

"You heading to N'Awlins?" Sheriff Atkins asked.

Interesting that her mother hadn't told him. "Nope, New York City. Manhattan to be precise. I'm also looking into colleges."

Sheriff Atkins said, "Going to school, are you? Good for you."

"Yes," Nell said, unable to keep the excitement out of her voice. "I'm going to college." She said that more for herself than for conversation, making the idea more real.

"What are you studying?" Sheriff Atkins asked.

"Everything." A small thrill swept through her. She had so much lost time to make up for. She wanted to know all she could learn. "But I haven't picked a major yet. I thought I'd see what I'm interested in."

"My baby," Lucy said with a grin, "is really smart. She needs to use that brain God gave her."

A spurt of anger rose in Nell and she stood. They needed to talk. "Mama, can I have a word with you in the office? I want you to help me with next week's order."

"Sure, just let me finish here."

Nell tapped her fingers on the countertop, trying to control her impatience. "Now, please."

Lucy looked surprised, but she nodded briefly. As she followed Nell into the office, she said, "That was downright rude, Nell. I thought my mama taught you better manners than that. What will Sheriff Atkins think of you?"

Nell whirled around. "Somehow, somewhat, if he's as smart as I think he is, he'll probably thank me for saving him from your clutches."

"My clutches!" Lucy's eyebrows rose and she looked a little hurt.

"I heard the rumors. All through high school, you dragged that poor man around like he had a ring in his nose. And when something better came along, you dumped him and moved on with your life."

Lucy looked sad. "I was a child back then. And I

realize what I did in my past is nothing to be proud of. Maybe I'm trying to make amends. I did apologize and asked him if he could forgive me."

"And maybe you're just bored and need some entertaining in our backwater town, and you think that nice man is going to provide it for you."

Lucy stopped still and stared at Nell. "You're being hurtful, Nell. You've never been hurtful before. I hope all that money isn't going to your head."

Nell clenched her fists. Her mother was right, but at the moment she didn't care. "How much? Just tell me how much money it will take for you to get lost forever."

Lucy tugged on her apron as she stared at her feet. "Maybe I want something more than money."

"Like what?" Nell rested her hands on her hips, fighting her anger. She didn't think she had anything else to give her mother that she might want.

Lucy raised her head and looked Nell square in the eye, a fat tear rolling down her cheek. "Your time. Your respect. Your love. Your forgiveness."

Nell froze, not understanding. She didn't know what to say, but to have her mother want forgiveness was such a surprise she didn't know how to respond. Her eyes narrowed. Was Lucy playing her now? What the hell was her angle? Though her gut instinct told her Lucy was being sincere, Nell didn't want that from her mother. She wanted to hang on to her anger, and seeing Lucy in a bad light was easier than forgiving her. Forgiving her meant opening the gates

to all sorts of possibilities Nell didn't want to explore. "I have to go," Nell said.

"You think about what I said, Nell."

Nell turned around to say no, but her mother's
next words stopped her.

"I love you, Nell. I always have."

Nell clamped her mouth shut and rushed out of
the office. She crossed the diner determined to get
out as quickly as possible, but Larry Drake, who
owned the biggest car dealership in the South, according to his advertising, stepped in front of her
before she could escape.

Larry thrust a bouquet of daisies at her. "Nell, can
I talk to you?"

Nell stopped to stare at him. Larry Drake was a
handsome enough man with perfectly tanned skin,
striking blue eyes and slicked-back blond hair, but
she could see the dollar signs in his eyes. He smiled
at her. His teeth were too white and too shiny as
though he'd coated them in Vaseline. As nice as the
wrapping might be on the outside, she figured on the
inside the box was empty.

"What do you want, Larry?" she asked, taking in his
powder-blue suit, white shirt and dark blue power tie.

"Has anyone ever told you that you're a beautiful woman?" he asked.

Made more so by eighteen million bucks. "Denzel
Washington calls me up every day to tell me I'm
beautiful and I get e-mails from Brad Pitt every
other day."

Larry gave a hollow laugh that sort of sounded sincere but was a little too high-pitched. "I've always liked a woman with a sense of humor."

And a big bank account, Nell thought. "I can see that about you." Nell crossed her arms over her chest and waited.

He reached out and touched her upper arm. "You and I would make a spectacular team."

Nell took a step back or else she would have slapped him. *Yes,* she thought. *I give you the money and you spend the money. I'd be broke in no time. Five years, tops.* "I've never thought about you and I as a team."

He moved closer to her and slid a hand around her to pat her butt. Nell pushed his hand away. "I haven't given you permission to touch me."

"Just hinting of some of the fringe benefits if you and I partner up together."

"Really," Nell said.

He moved in close enough for her to smell the peppermint on his breath. "Oh yeah!"

Okay, she'd had enough. She pushed him away and turned to the almost-full diner and shouted, "Attention, everyone. Attention, please."

Everyone stopped eating and looked up at her. She took a big breath. "For all you single men who have now found me and my millions dateable— forget about it. You couldn't ask me out when I was poor fat Nell, so don't even think about asking me out now that I'm rich fat Nell. I'm not that desper-

ate. And for your information, I never have been."
She whirled around, shoved Larry out of the way and
stamped out the door. If she could have slammed it,
she would have.

She marched down the street without looking
back.

She walked to Riley's house, a ham, macaroni and
cheese casserole and a peach pie in the basket looped
over her arm. She'd spent all afternoon cooking
because the offering of food was the only way she
knew to apologize to Riley. She'd had no idea how
raw his feelings still were.

She rang the doorbell and he opened it.

He looked haggard and tired. "Nell. What are you
doing here?"

She held out the basket and smiled. "I brought
you a peace offering."

He looked at the basket without taking it. "You
didn't have to cook for me."

"I'm a Southern girl. I only know how to apologize with food."

He chuckled and her confidence went up a notch.
She stepped closer to the door.

He sniffed the air. "What do you have in there?"

"Some of your favorites. Ham, macaroni and
cheese casserole." She held the basket higher. "I
even threw in some broccoli for healthy eating."

He grinned at her. "You have to have the four
basic food groups."

Relief flooded her. "And peach pie. Big Leroy at the bakery gave me his recipe after I swore a blood oath not to tell anybody how he makes it."

"You're not gonna have to date Big Leroy, are you?"

She shook her head. "He's happily married, and Gail scares me."

Riley was grinning broadly now. He stood inside and waved her in. "I heard about what happened in the diner this afternoon."

"Yeah," she said as she headed to the kitchen and placed her basket on the counter. She opened a cabinet and took out a dish for him. "I had one of those mother-daughter conversations and I think it made me a little nutty. I took it out on Larry Drake."

"Join me," Riley suggested at the sight of the one plate.

"Thanks, Riley." She took another plate down and set the table quickly. Then she pulled the casserole out of the basket and set it in the center of the table.

"Tell me about your talk with your mama." He was trying to avoid talking about what had happened at the cemetery.

"Before I do that, I need to apologize for what happened this morning." A flash of pain crossed his face, but Nell went on, needing to get her feelings off her chest. "Whether I agree with you or not, what you feel is what you feel. I should have gotten the hint sooner."

He gave her a searching look, nodded, and sat down. He picked up his fork. "Apology accepted."

She studied him. His acceptance came a little too quickly, but she would take what he would give her. She would be leaving town soon, and getting too enmeshed into his personal problems would make her feel even more guilty. She didn't like the idea that she would be abandoning him to deal with his problems on his own, but she had promised herself she would leave Wayloo with a clean slate and taking on his pain wasn't going to work for her. As much as she hurt for him, dreams had to come first.

She sat down and spooned macaroni onto her plate.

"So," Riley said, "tell me what happened at the diner."

"What did you hear?" She kept her voice light. "And who did you hear it from?"

"Chloe stopped by this afternoon. She heard the gossip from Linda Hoyt who heard it from her boyfriend, Deputy Baker, who heard it directly from Sheriff Atkins, who I believe was a witness."

"That's a reliable chain of gossip. So I don't have to straighten out the details since the source is so trustworthy. Good thing they didn't listen in on my conversation with my mother. Boy, would the tongues be wagging then. I don't know what to do about her."

"What's going on?"

Nell piled her plate with the cheesy noodles. "She

breezes back into my life and thinks she can have a relationship with me now that my grandmother is dead. She's spent her whole life pretending I don't exist, and now that I have all the money, she wants to be my buddy as if the past doesn't matter."

"Tell her to leave. You can say who stays in your house."

"But some part of me sees her as sad. As though she regrets something. I just don't know what that is."

"What is she saying to you?"

"She wants me to respect her, love her and forgive her." Okay, that didn't sound as bad now as it did earlier.

"Why can't you do that?" Riley asked.

She thought a moment. Why couldn't she? She didn't have to give her mother her address after she moved. "Because I don't want to hope again. I spent my childhood waiting for her to come back, praying for her to come back and love me. But every time she showed up, she'd stay a day or two and then would be on her way again. She'd chuck me under the chin, tell me to be a good girl and respect grand-mama. I did those things a dutiful daughter does, and what did it get me?"

"Eighteen-point-five million dollars, honey," Riley supplied.

Well duh. "Yeah, and marriage proposals from every Tom, Dick and Bubba within fifty miles who doesn't already have a ring on his finger. And I tell you what. If ninety percent of the women in this town didn't own guns, I'd probably be getting propositions from *their* husbands. Poor Larry, I just unloaded on him. He is sleazy and smarmy and all those nasty things, but I dropped a load of shit on him. He's like all the rest of them. They don't think I'm smart enough to figure out their plan—or that if I *was* dumb enough to accept their proposal I wouldn't insist on a damn prenuptial agreement."

"Nell, you're cussing. Twice in one minute." Riley looked so surprised she almost laughed. "I don't know whether to be impressed or shocked."

"I'm getting ready for New York City. I need a good potty mouth." Though the idea of cussing made her squirm. Grandmama would never approve and Pastor Willis would look at her with such disappointment in having wasted so many Sundays on her soul. "And now everyone in five counties is going to know what happened at the diner today."

"That's gonna mean one of two things," Riley said with a laugh. "Every single man is going to stop proposing, or you're going to get a lot of out-of-towners."

"Small towns, they never change," she said, and though she joined into his laughter, she thought about how everyone knew what everyone was doing. "I'm looking forward to anonymity." And the knowledge that if she did something someone disapproved of, fifty people wouldn't be calling her grandmother to complain. She could remember as a child, if she did something—*anything*—by the time she'd pedaled home on her bike, a half-dozen people would have called her grandmama to complain about her behavior.

"When I first moved to Chicago," Riley said, "I figured people not knowing my past was a good thing. But when I really needed help, I had no community to turn to. Chloe and I only had each other. Which is one of the reasons why we moved back to town. I discovered I'd rather be in a small town than a big, impersonal city."

"Not me," Nell said as she dug into the macaroni. "Nobody knows anything about me unless I want them to know. Nobody will ever judge me because they are too busy minding their own business. I get to be a whole new person, the Nell Evans I always wanted to be."

"You can do that here." Riley ate the macaroni and his face lit up.

"No, I can't," she replied. "Now, I'm rich Nell and every single man is looking for a meal ticket, and every woman is looking to see if I'll go crazy after inheriting all this money. But when I move to New York City, no one is going to know I have money unless I want them to. Or whether I'm crazy or not."

"Nell, that sounds a little sad."

She didn't think so. "Why so?"

"I can't put my finger on it exactly. Maybe not sad, maybe *lonely* is a better word."

"One thing I read in *Cosmo* magazine is that

you're only as lonely as you want to be. And I figure, I'm gonna be way too busy with school and I'll just get a little side job to fill my time. I'm gonna get along fine in the big city. I just know it."

"Nell, you'll be whatever you want to be."

Yeah, now that I have the means to be that person. And leaving Wayloo was the first step. She felt a tingle of excitement, mixed with a little fear, running through her. She was embarking on the greatest adventure of her life and some mornings she could hardly wait.

After Nell left, Riley went out on the back porch and stood watching evening shadows fill the yard as the sun set. A cool breeze played with the leaves on the live oaks. And the strained trickle of water from his fountain told him the filter needed changing again. He had no flowers, preferring bushes, trees and grass. He watched Chester make his rounds to said bushes.

But he wondered what flowers he would like. Nell liked flowers.

He didn't like the men who hovered around Nell proposing to her and making a nuisance of themselves. Where were their brains? Did they really think she was that dumb? He could almost laugh, but something about Nell made him feel protective of her.

As much as he liked the new Nell, he did miss the old one. She was more self-confident now. Had it only been two days ago when she'd marched up his driveway with the offer of her virginity? She was like a sweet little kitten just let off her leash who had turned into a big, bad tiger. Suddenly, she was sexy, and he liked the confident new Nell. He had always been attracted to women who were confident about themselves; it was one of the things that had attracted him to Chloe.

And now Nell was growing up and becoming the woman he'd always envisioned she would be. He wanted to rush right over to her house and start the process of seduction all over again. But then he remembered he already had her permission to seduce her.

He should just have swept her off her feet when he and Chloe had divorced, instead of settling for what they had, a nice safe friendship. He'd waited too long to make his move and now he would lose her.

Damn! He wanted her, but he knew he wasn't capable of loving her the way she needed to be loved. He didn't think he was capable of giving his heart again. Especially after today. The sight of Benjy's grave had proved he hadn't moved on, just buried the pain deeper.

But a part of him wanted to try. If only he had the time.

Chapter 8

Nell loved the Escalade the moment she sat down in the supple leather seats. "Maybe I should get one of these instead of the Mini Cooper," she said, then she thought about preserving her inheritance. "No, I have to think about gas prices and the environment." She ran her hand over the buttery leather and tried not to sigh too loudly.

Chloe laughed. "If we'd had this swanky ride when we were married, I would have made sure I got it in the divorce settlement."

Riley shook his head. "Thank you for reminding me why I'm not marrying you again. You've turned out to be one greedy woman."

Chloe laughed again.

Nell couldn't help but admire Chloe. Her ability to ease stressful situations was something Nell would like to have.

Chloe wore a simple green dress that set off her dusky skin. A sun hat perched on her head, shading her face. Nell felt dowdy in her old patched jeans and a yellow T-shirt sporting the diner's logo on the back. She'd opted for comfort and easy to get in and out of.

The Escalade purred like the luxury car it was. Nell crossed her legs and leaned back into the cushiony softness. This was what having money was like—luxury. She'd never had luxury in her entire life. She wasn't going to the beauty shop, but the salon. She wasn't going to buy her clothes anymore at the Wal-Mart or at Doolittle's, but at a classy boutique or an upscale department store. She intended to change more than just her life, but what went on inside her.

Excitement coursed through her. Today was the start of the rest of her life.

New York City—here I come!

For the first time in her life, Nell wasn't buying her clothes based on cost. She looked at herself in the full-length mirror. The silky black halter dress she wore hugged her curves and made her feel desirable. But as beautiful as the dress made her feel, she couldn't seem to forget Riley. And each dress she selected made her wonder if he would be turned on by her choice.

The exclusive New Orleans boutique was situated on Magazine Street, tucked between a rare bookshop and an antique store. The minute Nell had entered, she'd fallen in love with the place. The muted interior, decorated in tones of cream and gold, had mannequins casually placed around the store to showcase the elegant clothing that hung on hangers from the racks.

The place was so tasteful, so elegantly understated, she almost forgot to check the price tags. When she did, she tried not to gasp and show her country roots. Who was it that once said, "If you have to ask the price, you can't afford it"?

In her whole life, Nell had never paid more than twenty-five dollars for a dress, and in this shop, the dresses were in the hundreds and a few even cost a over a thousand dollars. Her fingers trembled at the prices even as she longed to try on a chic red suit that she knew would look stunning on her.

Chloe was in her element. She and the shop's owner knew each other and the owner had greeted Chloe with air-kisses and gushing praise. For the first time, Nell realized that Chloe's clothes came from this shop. And yet Chloe never looked overdressed. Elegant, expensive, stylish and always comfortable, Nell wondered what her secret was.

She studied herself in the three-sided mirrors. She hadn't known she had it in her to look this pretty. For the first time in her life, she thought she wasn't so fat, she was... What did Riley call her?

Voluptuous. Yes, that was the word. She liked that word. She was going to think of herself as voluptuous from now on.

Nell had to have this dress. Who ever thought shopping could be so much fun? She thought of the boxes and bags already piling up in the back of the Escalade. She'd never had a wardrobe so beautiful or expensive before. She felt a little guilty spending her grandmother's…no, her money, so easily, but how could she argue with a dress that made her butt look this sexy?

"How you doing, Nell?" Chloe asked through the dressing-room door.

She opened the door and the old doubts came back for a visit. "I'm not sure."

Chloe took a step back and ran a practiced look over Nell. "You look fabulous. I really like you in black."

Pursing her lips, she stared down at her cleavage. "You think I can go sleeveless? Aren't my arms too wiggly?"

Chloe laughed. "With that neckline and that cleavage, who is going to notice your arms, dear?"

Nell could only smile. Their first stop of the morning had been at Victoria's Secret and the lacy blue bra and matching panties made her feel so sexy and so attractive. "I love this dress, but I've just never had anything…so…so…" She didn't know what to say. "My grandmother would never have allowed me to wear a dress like this."

"Your grandmother was a dictator. She was so afraid you'd end up like your mother she kept you on a tight leash. You never had a chance to find out who you were."

Everything Chloe said was true. "I know all that."

"Well, hon, you've blossomed. I'm not quite sure I understand why you want to go and take a bite out of the Big Apple, but I say, more power to you. You have taken charge of your life."

Nell whirled back to the mirror and stared at herself. She fingered the silk fabric and thought about how fine the dress was, how it showed off her cleavage to her advantage and actually made her look curvy and not big. For the first time ever she even thought she looked attractive. "Do you think Riley will like it?"

Chloe rolled her eyes. "Any man with a pulse would like you in that dress."

Nell laughed, still not believing Chloe was all right with helping her transform. "This really doesn't bother you?"

"My wish is for him to find happiness again. He's really closed himself off from life."

"Sometimes he looks so sad. I always wished…" She remembered the scene at the cemetery and how much pain he'd been in. She had caused that pain.

"What did you wish, Nell?"

"That I could help him somehow. I don't know what I'm trying to say."

"He has to want your help," Chloe said sadly.

"How do I get him to do that?"

"Do I look that smart?" Chloe sat down on the powder-blue chair in the corner.

Nell tugged at the dress, suddenly feeling uncomfortable in the warm silk. "I've known you for a long time, and of all the pretty, popular kids in Wayloo, you were never smug about who you were. You were always nice to everybody. I know you tried to be my friend in high school, but my own insecurities and not being willing to trust my own judgment made me push you away. And I want to say, I'm sorry. I wish we could have those days back again."

"I wasn't so different from you. Being popular was my way of combating my own insecurities just like every other girl. Some people hide, some people make friends with everybody and some people are bitches."

Chloe's gaze met Nell's and they both said, "Wanda Dobbs." Nell started to laugh and Chloe covered her mouth.

"Do you know what happened to Wanda Dobbs?" Nell asked.

"Haven't seen her in years." Chloe crossed her legs. "Don't really care."

Nell didn't gossip and she'd been holding on to this tidbit for a long time. She was dying to tell someone. "She ended up a porn star with about fifty thousand dollars in plastic surgery and now she looks like a Siamese cat. She calls herself Mimi Cummin."

"You're kidding!" Chloe eyes went wide.

"Kid you not," Nell replied. "She came home a

year before you and Riley moved back to settle her affairs after her mom passed. She left so fast she forgot to pay the last month's rent and my grandmother and I went to clean out the place and I found some of her movies on VHS."

"Oh, my God. Little Miss Choir Girl a porn star." Chloe leaned forward. "Did you watch them?"

Nell licked her lips. Her entire face got hot, just remembering some of the things Wanda Dobbs had done with all those men. "Just a few minutes. Enough to know she put her double-jointedness to good use. But I was so embarrassed I threw them away. I'm sure some man at the dump thought he'd hit the jackpot. Every once in a while I look her up online, following her career. She's very popular."

"I guess she's not coming back for our class's tenth reunion in three years." Chloe snapped her fingers. "Damn, that would have been great to let that one drop at a critical moment."

Nell just laughed.

"Aren't you going to miss small-town life?" Chloe asked.

"Never. Don't you miss living in the big city?"

Chloe shrugged. "The big city is just so impersonal. But I will admit, I do miss having a Starbucks on practically every corner." She sighed. "Maybe I ought to check into buying a franchise. Do you think fancy coffee would play in Wayloo? Can you imagine Luther Troy Riggs asking for a mocha nonfat extra-hot extra-whip?"

Nell chuckled. "No."

A light knock sounded on the door of the dressing room. Nell, thinking it was the saleswoman, flung open the door to find Riley standing outside.

"Riley, what are you doing here?"

His gaze swept up and down her body, an appreciative glint in his dark brown eyes. "Just wanted to see how things are progressing."

"Everything is progressing just fine," Nell said. She whirled for him and saw his eyes linger on her breasts and then her hips.

"Yes, I can see that it is." He pursed his lips and whistled. "Nice. Very nice." Again his eyes lingered on her cleavage.

Nell felt an irrational desire to cover her chest with her hands, which was something the old Nell would do, not the new Nell. She struck a pose; she was big-city, bold Nell. "I'm glad you like it."

"*Like* is not the word I would have used. More like..." he paused, his head tilted to one side "...*sizzling*. I'm taking you and that dress out for a night on the town."

Chloe's cell phone rang and she answered it. When she hung up, she said, "That was my aunt Nicole, she's picking me up in twenty minutes. I forgot to tell you that I'm having dinner with her and spending the night." Chloe gave Nell a penetrating look and jiggled her perfectly arched eyebrows. "You can pick me up in the morning when you're ready to leave."

For a second Nell didn't know what the look meant, then realized that tonight was probably the night she and Riley would get down to business. She felt heat rise up her throat to her cheeks. Nell didn't know what to say.

Chloe picked up her purse and slipped past Riley, whose gaze never left Nell. "I'll leave you two to finish up." And she was gone.

Riley swallowed. "I wasn't planning on spending the night." He couldn't take his gaze off Nell. She looked fabulous in the saucy black dress. Suddenly, he wanted to get her alone so he could touch and fondle and finish what they'd started the other day. Her lessons had been neglected the last couple of days, between her mother's arrival and just the chaos of life, and he wanted to get them going again.

Nell licked her luscious lips. "I didn't think you'd planned this."

The memory of her lips on his sent his pulse into hyperdrive. How could she look so demure and so uninhibited at the same time?

He pushed a curl back from her face. His fingers lingered for an extra moment on the smoothness of her cheek. Heat rose, threatening to scorch him. This was his Nell, the woman he'd lusted after even in her concealing waitress uniform. And here she was turning into a sophisticated woman and he wanted her even more.

"I'm taking you out to dinner tonight," he said. "Where do you want to go?"

She smiled sweetly at him. "I've always wanted to go to Brennan's."

"It's a date. Why don't you finish up here and I'll go rent us a couple of rooms at the Bienville Hotel."

"That's a very elegant place. But you're only going to rent one room." She held up one finger.

His mouth dropped open. His felt the heat start to really boil. "You mean…tonight."

She shrugged. "Why not? We're having no luck at either my house or your house."

Now he was having doubts. Hell, he was having performance anxiety. When was the last time that happened to him? "But…I'm not sure I'm ready for this tonight."

She gave him a long, steady gaze. "Tonight is the night, Riley."

When did she become the seductress? He could feel his heart speeding up with anticipation and dread. Once the final deed was committed, she wouldn't have any reason to stay. Once he'd fulfilled his part of the bargain, she'd be ready to move on to her new life.

He knew he'd agreed to teach her all the ins and outs of romance and sex, but he found himself in a quandary. He knew he wanted to make love to her, but he didn't know if he was ready. Which amazed him, considering how confused he felt. Actually, he wasn't certain what he felt. He'd never put so much

thought and energy into seduction since his marriage. Usually he took out a woman knowing they'd
have a good time and part on easy terms at the end
of the evening. There would be no easy parting with
Nell. She wasn't the love 'em and leave 'em kind of
girl his other women had been. "If you're sure you're
ready." Lame, lame, lame.

"You still want to do this, right?" Nell asked.

"Yeah! Why do you ask?"

Nell snapped her fingers in front of his eyes a
couple of times. "I kind of lost you there for a couple
seconds."

"And I can tell you this because we're friends, but
I want you to know I'm breaking a man rule here."

Her eyes went wide. "What?"

"I'm having a little performance anxiety here."

Her mouth fell open and she stared at him. "Only
you will know if your performance is bad or not. I'm
a rank beginner."

"For my first time I had no expectations. I was
just happy to get there."

"What if I lie still like a dead halibut?" Suddenly, Nell started giggling. She covered her
mouth with her hands.

Is she laughing at me or with me? Riley couldn't
tell, though he had to admit his own amusement at
the odd situation they were in. "Let's just start with
a nice dinner and we'll see what happens."

"Get over your anxiety. Take my packages to the car,
buy some condoms. Do what you need to do to prepare

yourself for this evening. I'm going to buy some more lingerie." She pushed him out of the dressing room and closed the door with a snap. "Go, Riley."

He almost launched himself toward the door, passing Chloe who stood at the lingerie counter holding up a skimpy black thong bikini. Her cell phone was pressed to her ear. She glanced at him. "Do you like?" she asked.

"Oh yeah!" he said as he pushed through the door to the street.

Riley nursed a whiskey at the bar across the street and down a block from the hotel as he waited for Nell. Tonight was the night.

They were finally going to do it.

His palms were sweating. Damn, he hadn't been this nervous his first time. He checked his watch; she was five minutes late. *Not very Nell-like,* he thought to himself.

He felt someone's eyes on him. He turned slightly to his left and spotted an attractive brunette in the back booth giving him a come-hither smile.

He smiled back at her.

She patted the empty spot next to her and he shook his head and turned back to face the mirrored wall of the bar.

Five days ago, he would have been stalking the brunette fast enough, but today she didn't even raise his pulse. He had Nell. Just as he'd always wanted. Just as he'd always dreamed about. Of course it was only going to be for a little while. Long enough, he hoped, to get her out of his system, but he wasn't going to bet on that. She was a fever in his blood.

He felt more like a man than he'd ever felt before. How did she do that to him? Hell, how did he let her do that to him? He didn't feel like a weakling. Hell no, this felt right. Like it was supposed to feel.

He'd never felt this way with Chloe. With Chloe, everything was nice, safe, secure. But Nell made his world shake and explode. He was off-kilter all the time. And the worst thing was that he found he liked the sensation.

Lifting the glass to his lips, he intended to drain it, but he caught a flash of black in the mirror. He swung around on the bar stool and saw Nell standing in the doorway looking a little uncomfortable. She saw him and tottered over on her brand-new black high heels that made her legs look extra-long and so sweet and curvy he was ready to jump her bones right there in the bar.

She wore the saucy black dress. Dare he hope she wore a black thong? Oh please, please, please. He'd never ask for anything else in life again. Okay, maybe he wanted to see it, too. And to touch it. And to take it off. There, that would be enough. He'd be satisfied. She smiled at him, her full lips tilting into a sensuous curve.

Chapter 9

"Wow, you look great." Riley took her hand and slipped it around his arm. Her skin was soft beneath his fingers and he could smell the musky perfume she'd purchased earlier. He was going to spend the whole evening forcing himself to behave until they returned to the hotel. Then all bets were off.

She flushed in the muted light. "Thank you, but I owe it all to Chloe. She really understands what makes a woman look good. Even a woman like me."

"Chloe has good taste. A knack for spending money, but she only did a bit of redecorating. She had a lot to work with." He left a tip under his glass for the waitress and guided Nell out of the bar and out onto the street.

She gave him a smile that just about rocked him to his core. Even though he and Chloe hadn't been able to keep their marriage together, he considered himself lucky to have known her. But with Nell, he was beyond lucky. She was good fortune at its best.

The evening sun cast long shadows on the banquette sidewalks. New Orleans never lost its magic. Heavy humidity hung over the city. By morning, pools of water would dot the sidewalks. A horse and carriage passed, the people inside craning their necks to look at something the driver pointed out. The heat of the day had eased a little, and traffic on Decatur was light, but pedestrian traffic was heavy. Vendors still lined the wrought-iron fences enclosing Jackson Square, hawking their paintings, T-shirts, jewelry or offering tarot-card readings.

"How is it that you and Chloe are still the best of friends?" Nell asked as they walked along the side of Jackson Square. He'd thought about hailing a taxi, but Brennan's was only two blocks away.

Every woman in Wayloo he'd dated always asked this question; he should be used to it. "Nell, honey, a good rule of thumb for dating—if a man talks a lot about his ex-wife, he's still got issues and you should avoid him at all costs."

She fumbled with her evening purse, snapping it open and pulling out her journal and pen. She made a few scribbles on the paper as they walked.

"You're taking notes?" he asked.

She nodded. "Well, yes. I realized there is so

much to know that I needed to take notes, so I bought this notebook. Some of the dating information is overwhelming." She flipped over the cover and riffled the pages, showing him what she'd written.

What he wouldn't give to get good long peek at the notebook. "Have you been taking notes on everything?"

"I am now. Shouldn't I?"

He picked up a few words, but she closed the notebook and pen, putting them back in her evening purse. "Are you going to write a research paper?" he asked.

"No," she laughed, "but I do like to study what we've done and how I felt about it."

Now that made him feel kind of strange. "What about our picnic? Did that make it into your notes?"

"Of course."

His palms started to sweat. What if someone found her notebook. "Do you have to do that?"

"Yes." She shrugged and gave him an inquisitive glance. "How do you expect me to get better at this dating and sex thing if I don't study?"

Well, that made sense in a twisted sort of way, but he still felt odd thinking about her analyzing his every move as a lover and putting her thoughts down in that little book. "What if someone finds your notebook?"

"I have a sort of shorthand that I use."

He was grateful for that. "Why do that?"

She blew out a long breath. "I knew my grandmother used to read my diary, and so I learned to do this so she couldn't understand it."

His father couldn't have cared less what he did and her grandmother cared too much. They were a perfect pair. "I'm sorry you had to grow up hiding so much."

"Don't be." She patted his arm. "My grandmother was a sad, lonely woman. I understand why she was the way she was and I forgive her."

She brushed against him as she tottered in her high heels and he felt instant heat spreading through him. "Why didn't you try to leave?"

"She needed me. And I didn't know how to break free. I was too afraid."

What do you say about something like that? "You were smart, you got good grades and could have gone to college. The teachers would have helped you."

A tear slipped down her cheek. "I don't think this is good date conversation, do you?" She gave him a shaky smile. "I've been watching baseball. Don't most men like to talk about sports?"

"What do you like to talk about?"

"I don't really have much to talk about. I haven't had much of a life outside of work or church."

"What do you intend to do in New York City?" *Besides find yourself some guy to get cozy with.*

"I've applied to college. I don't think I'll have any trouble getting into NYU, Fordham or Columbia. My grades were good and I scored high on my

SAT's. And the fact that I have a lot of liquid assets doesn't hurt, either. I think I want to be a teacher or maybe a lawyer. Right now I just want to take a lot of different subjects and learn about everything I don't know. Which is a lot."

He knew it was probably useless, but he couldn't help himself from trying to talk her out of leaving. They were just getting to know each other and he wanted this to continue. "You don't have to go so far. There's Tulane, Xavier, Old Dominion. That's three great colleges right here in spitting distance of home."

"New Orleans is just like Wayloo, only it's a little bigger. People are still in your business. People come here all the time from Wayloo to shop or do the shows at the casinos. Or just generally to get in trouble. I want to experience something completely different, and what could be more different than living in Manhattan?"

That's how he'd felt the second he'd found out he was accepted to the University of Chicago. "New York or bust, huh?"

"I want to go off and have my big adventure. Didn't you want a big adventure when you left Wayloo?"

"Yes, you do have a point." He'd had no idea that what he wanted was right in his hometown. "But I did eventually figure out that the greatest adventure can be found in your own backyard."

"For some people," she said.

"But not for you?"

She shook her head. "I really like this dress."

Ah, the old change-of-subject technique. He could go for that. "This dress screams big-city seductress to me." Since they'd taken to the street, he had noticed several men giving her the eye. But she seemed oblivious.

She giggled. "I feel really sexy in it."

"You look really sexy in it." Hot. Luscious. Delectable. He didn't know enough adjectives to describe how she looked. "So tell me, are you wearing a black thong also?"

She didn't answer.

"Come on, Nell, tell me," he asked softly.

She arched her eyebrows flirtatiously. "Wouldn't you like to know."

His jaw fell open at her remark just as they approached Brennan's. She sashayed inside and as the maître d' led them to their table, he noticed that half the men in the room turned to watch Nell as she threaded her way through the tables.

Once they'd been settled at their table, a waiter asked them if they wanted cocktails.

"A Cosmopolitan, please," Nell ordered.

"Are you sure?" Riley asked. "You're not much of a drinker." He knew her grandmother occasionally served wine at Sunday dinner, but he doubted Nell had much tolerance for alcohol.

She waved away his objections. "I have to build up my tolerance. I don't want to be a pushover. Except where you're concerned."

"Gee thanks, I think." An odd feeling crept over him and for a moment, he didn't recognize it. He mulled it over before realizing he was jealous of all the men in her future who would experience her vivaciousness, her charm, her innocent sexiness. The more he thought about her leaving, the more he wanted to talk her out of going. But he couldn't.

If anyone had tried to talk him into staying in Wayloo back in the day, he would have straight-up not listened. He'd been as eager to leave as she was. How could he stop her from going, when he'd done the same thing? She needed to go. She needed to find out there was more to life than their little corner of the world. He'd left to discover what he was made of, and she needed to find out the same thing, even more so because she'd been forced to stay.

Their drinks came. She took an experimental sip of the Cosmopolitan. Her lips curved up in a satisfying smile. "This is absolutely everything I thought it would be."

Riley had never seen anybody get so excited over a cocktail before. The waiter took their order. Salads to start. Nell bit her lips as she tried to choose her entrée and finally managed to settle on shrimp Victoria. Riley ordered blackened redfish. He was delighted when she asked for bananas Foster for desert, the specialty of the restaurant, and Riley's favorite desert.

"And may I suggest—" the waiter consulted the wine menu "—a nice chardonnay with your meal?"

.Nell agreed too quickly.

Riley didn't have the heart to say no, but he worried a little about the wine mixed with the Cosmopolitan. She wasn't a drinker, and he wanted to keep this night open to all possibilities, especially ones he wouldn't be able to enjoy with a drunk woman.

All through dinner, Nell was animated, chatty and vivacious. Riley observed her with a detached part of himself that seemed to have stepped to one side and watched from a distance. She giggled a little too much and Riley could tell that one Cosmopolitan and two glasses of wine had gone to her head. Maybe he'd better just take her back to the hotel and pour some hot coffee down her, but she was having so much fun.

A wave of guilt washed over him. She was having an adventure that probably seemed to her the start of the rest of her life. Who was he to put the brakes on it?

As she chatted and ate, Riley found himself thinking about her grandmother. With a grandmother like Sarah Evans, who could have real fun? Miz Sarah had been thin to the point of gauntness, tall and gradually more stooped as she'd aged. She'd had a stillness about her that used to make Riley avoid her as much as possible. Her dark, observant eyes had never missed anything. And he always felt like a bug under a magnifying glass in her presence.

And when Miz Sarah had offered to help him pay for his college, he'd been thunderstruck. He remembered her saying that few people in life surprised her, but he was one of them. Riley had been unable to comprehend her offer, but after thinking about it he knew nothing like this would ever happen again. And nothing would keep him in Wayloo, not even his pride. So he'd left, gotten his education, and with his and Chloe's first jobs, he'd paid Miz Sarah back every penny with interest. Although Benjy never went without, Riley and Chloe ate a lot of peanut butter and jelly sandwiches to get out from under that loan.

Which made him wonder why Miz Sarah would offer him an education, yet keep Nell tethered to her. He could understand Nell's anger. But he couldn't understand Miz Sarah. She'd been larger than life and so in control of everything around her.

Half the people who'd watched Lucy grow up and turn bad, never once blamed Miz Sarah. They thought Lucy was just a bad seed or had a few screws loose. But seeing Nell, he began to realize Miz Sarah had been afraid of things no one could comprehend. Whatever her fears, they had colored her perspective, making her cling to Nell long after she should have let go.

He watched as Nell tasted every bit of her food with such relish, he almost laughed.

"I've never eaten in a world-class restaurant before. The food really is better when you pay a lot of money for it." Nell pointed her fork at Riley's fish. "May I have a bite of your fish?"

Riley pushed his plate toward her. "Be my guest." He'd spent so much time watching her simple enjoyment, he'd forgotten to eat and no longer had an appetite.

Nell speared a piece of fish and forked it into her mouth. He watched her luscious lips curve around the morsel of fish and he reflected on the number of women he'd dated who'd pushed their food around their plates, ate a few bites and said they were done.

Nell relished her food. "That is wonderful!"

Actually watching her eat was heavenly.

She stopped eating, her fork half-raised. "You're staring at me. What's wrong?"

She was a little unfocused. He should have cut her off after the second sip of the Cosmopolitan. But he'd wanted her to have this experience. "I'm just enjoying watching you having fun."

She squinted one eye. "That's just odd."

"No, it's not."

She propped her chin on her hand. "I know this sounds bad, and if I didn't already have a glass of wine—or two—in me, I probably wouldn't say this, but…" Her voice lowered to a whisper and she leaned across the table toward him. "I've had more fun in the last three weeks since my grandmother died than I've had in my entire life."

Riley leaned over and whispered back, "It's okay, I understand."

Her eyes went wide and she burst out giggling. "That's good."

Riley laughed. The sight of her totally captivated him. And suddenly he wanted to get out of the restaurant and back to the hotel room and go on to the next step in their lessons.

"Let's take a carriage ride," Nell said after they left Brennan's and were walking through the French Quarter.

"Okay," he said, disappointed. But he would live; this was Nell's night to shine.

Music rocked the Quarter as Riley and Nell strolled hand-in-hand back toward their hotel. Nell couldn't keep her tension under control. This was it. This was the night she'd asked Riley for.

"We don't have to take a ride if you don't want to," Nell said. They could just get down to business. She wasn't expecting all the romance, too.

"Yes, I do," Riley said. "Do you want a man who takes you for carriage rides, or do you want a man who is honest with you? You need to know more than just sex, you need to know about dating."

"Like what?" She held her arms out wide. "We go out, have dinner, go to a movie and then have sex. What else is there to know?"

God, didn't she know how this was killing him? He didn't want her dating other men, much less sleeping with them. "Dating is how you get to know somebody."

"I already know you." She pointed her finger at him. "What's left to know about you?"

"I'm a complicated man. There are layers to me you have yet to dig up."

"Like what?" She tried not to think about the scene yesterday at the cemetery. She'd seen more to Riley in that moment than he realized he'd revealed to her.

"I like to go to museums."

"Really?" Nell said in surprise.

"I appreciate fine art." He sounded a little defensive.

"I'm not totally surprised. You worked as an architect."

"But you would never have found that out if we hadn't gone out on a date."

She gave his statement thought. True, but somehow dating seemed sort of old-fashioned in the fast-paced world of today. She gave him a long look. "Do you date the women you go out with, or do you just sleep with them?"

"What a question to ask a man." His laugh was a little shaky.

"Did you date Alice at the beauty parlor?"

"I took her to the movies."

"Was that before or after you had sex?" Nell had overheard a long conversation Alice had had with her sister Cathy one day when they'd come to the diner for lunch.

"Before."

She drummed her fingers. "What about Sally Mitchel?"

"Sex."

"Evelyn Rules?"

"Sex."

"Need I go on?"

"That's different. I'm the man." Another lame excuse, but it was the best he could come up with.

She stabbed his arm with the tip of her finger. "'I'm a man' is not an excuse. I don't know if I want to get married. Maybe all I want from the men I date is sex." Keeping relationships simple was one way of keeping sex simple, too.

"We both know you're not that kind of woman, Nell. Trust me, I know."

Her chin rose as if she were defending herself. "I may not be that kind of woman right now. But I could be. I'm going to New York with a blank slate, and I'm going to re-create myself and my life the way I want."

Did she get how scary that sounded? "That's fine if something's terribly wrong with your life, but I don't see your life as being wrong."

"Nothing's wrong?" she said with a sigh, uncertainty in her tone. "I'm boring. I've never done anything special in my whole life. In eight years, I've had two dates with two different men who took one look at my grandmother and never came back. I have been leading a life of quiet desperation."

Street musicians had taken over from the artists and tarot-card readers around Jackson Square. Lights trained on the cathedral lit it up against the dark sky. Couples strolled hand-in-hand as they meandered along the wrought-iron fence. The de Pontalba apartments, on the second floor over the shops that bordered the square, showed lights in the windows. One woman stood on her balcony and looked down at the street, a glass of wine in her hand.

Nell clung to Riley, her hand tucked around his elbow. "My feet hurt," she said. "I've never worn high heels for so long before. I don't know how Chloe does it. She wears them all day long and never seems to have tired feet." She stopped, bent over to adjust a strap on one shoe. When she straightened she wobbled, but Riley caught her and offered a steadying hand.

They walked toward the line of carriages. Nell stopped to pat a mule on its nose. "Let's take this one."

Riley dug into his pocket for the fare.

The driver helped Nell into the carriage and Riley stepped in after her. As the driver grinned at them and set his mule to a walk, Nell put her head on Riley's shoulder and sighed.

"This is the most romantic thing that has ever happened to me. This is the *only* romantic thing that's ever happened to me." She snuggled close to him and his heart thudded into overdrive. "Thank you, Riley."

He was thrilled, but a little sad for her that her whole life had been so sheltered, so devoid of the kind of excitement she craved. At the same time, he knew she could have left her grandmother at any time, but Nell was the kind of woman to whom loyalty and family were important. He admired that in her. And her grandmother had been kind enough to provide for her, for, if anything, Miz Sarah would know how to word her will to keep Nell tied to her beyond the grave. Whatever fears had guided Miz Sarah, she'd rewarded Nell's loyalty instead of chaining her for the rest of her life.

Riley settled back with Nell curled inside the curve of his arm. He couldn't help but think about the future men in her life and he hoped they appreciated the kind of woman she was. The carriage driver had a running monologue as he guided them through the French Quarter, but Riley wasn't paying attention. He'd heard it all before. He paid more attention to Nell and the way she smelled. He'd been thinking about having sex with her since he'd discovered his hormones.

The driver talked about ghosts and spurned wives and mistresses. The words washed right over Riley as he held Nell. He'd never really pursued a relationship with Nell. He'd taken a couple of steps with her, but she hadn't responded. Why didn't he go further, push harder? But deep inside, he'd always felt he wasn't quite good enough for Nell.

He felt the smoothness of her dress beneath his fingers. The heat of her body pressed against him. Her breath was like a soft summer breeze against his neck. He so ached for her. He flared into arousal and suddenly wanted the carriage ride over. Why had he let her talk him into it?

Nell gazed at the carriage driver, entranced by his little jokes and stories. Riley simply studied the buildings they passed. How long? How long? He wanted Nell alone, under him, with no mothers to break in on them, or kids ditching school at the swimming hole.

His foot thumped impatiently against the floor of the carriage. Come on! Come on! Be over! Be over!

Nell's eyes had closed. She'd gone limp and he knew she was asleep. When the carriage came to a stop, Riley smiled at the driver. "Again," he said in a low voice. He eased his wallet out of his pocket and the driver leaned forward and took the offered money. He grinned at Riley and instead of stopping, he pulled out of the line of carriages and started his route yet again, only this time without the stories and jokes.

Nell felt so good curled up against Riley. He didn't want the carriage ride to end. Never in his life had he done something so romantic, and he liked the feeling. With other women, he'd been romantic to get something, but with Nell he wanted romance for the sake of romance.

The night air was sultry with the faint scent of magnolia blossoms. The moon cast the street into silver shadows. The clopping of the mule's hooves added an hypnotic rhythm to the night. Riley leaned his head back and felt such contentment steal over him, he wanted the night to go on and on.

Finally, the carriage driver pulled up to the curb

at Jackson Square again. Riley roused Nell. She looked sweet and vulnerable with her sleep-fogged eyes. The driver helped Riley get her down and she stood on the banquette yawning.

Riley tipped the driver and then took Nell by the hand. "Let's get back to the hotel," he said.

She smiled at him, her eyes sparkling. She turned and went down with a thud. Riley reached for her, but when he tried to draw her up, she moaned and he sat her down on the banquette again. She held her ankle, her face drawn up in pain.

"Riley," she moaned, "I think I broke my ankle."

The bottom of his world dropped. *Yep, it was going to be a long night, and not in a good way.*

Chapter 10

Nell lay on a bed in a curtained cubicle waiting for the results of the X-ray and trying to decide what was worse—the pain in her ankle or the embarrassment. Riley hovered over her. He tried to look sympathetic, but she could see the disappointment in his eyes.

"Riley." She held a hand out to him. "I'm so sorry. I shouldn't have had all that wine. But it tasted so good."

He took her hand and lifted it to his lips. "Don't worry about it."

"But this was supposed to be our big night." Her head fell back against the stone-hard pillow.

"Nell," he said, holding her hand, massaging her skin, "stop worrying. We'll find another opportunity."

His fingers were warm on her and she felt a thrill course through her. "You can dress me up," she said, "but you can't make a silk purse out of a sow's ear." She covered her eyes with her free hand.

"What do you mean by that?" His dark eyes sparkled. And his grip on her hand tightened.

Nell cringed. He actually looked angry with her. "Here I am, some backwoods country girl trying to think she can take on the big city. Does this kind of thing happen to sophisticated women?"

"Nell," Riley soothed, "you're being too harsh on yourself. I've seen women trip in the same kind of stilts you're wearing without the aid of alcohol." His grip on her hand loosened. "This could have happened to anyone."

"I'm just country," she wailed.

Riley shook his head. "Hardly. Not in that dress. Not in those black silk thong bikinis you're wearing today."

"I was not particularly comfortable with where the thong was going, so I didn't wear them."

Riley looked shocked. "You mean you're wearing your granny panties under that gorgeous dress?"

"No," she said, shaking her head. "They ruined the line of the dress."

"What *are* you wearing?"

"Nothing. And I fell on the sidewalk." Her bare skin had touched concrete and she didn't like it.

"Nothing. You're wearing nothing under that dress."

She wiped away her tears. "What did you think I was wearing under the dress?"

He ran a hand down his face, and his eyes seemed to roll back in his head. For a second, Nell wondered if he was going to pass out cold on the emergency-room floor.

"Nell," he said, his voice thick and hoarse.

"Is something wrong, Riley?"

He put a hand on the side of the bed. "No," he said, his voice sounding strangled, "just trying not to think about some things."

"Like what?" She tried to push herself up, but the little movement sent shock waves of pain through her ankle.

He touched her fingers. "Nothing important. We need to get you taken care of and get you back to the hotel for a good night's sleep."

"You're mad at me, aren't you?"

"I can never be mad at you for long." He pinched the bridge of his nose with his free hand. "Right now, I'm just mad at the universe."

The doctor pushed aside the curtain and walked in. "Miss Evans, I have your X-rays." He held the X-rays in his hand. "The ankle isn't broken, just hyperextended. That's always a problem with stiletto heels." He bent over to gently prod her ankle. His hands were cool and dry on her skin. "But you'll be fine in a few days."

A nurse bustled in holding a contraption in her hand. When the doctor completed his exam, he left and the nurse started to wrap Nell's ankle in an elastic bandage. When she'd finished with the bandage, she fitted a removable cast over her foot and ankle.

By the time Riley got her back to the hotel, Nell was so tired she could barely keep her eyes open. She had painkillers in her purse for later, crutches to get around with, and she felt like a dismal failure.

In their room, Riley helped her out of her dress and into her nightgown with his eyes closed.

Nell watched him, puzzled. "You can open your eyes, Riley. It's not like you've never seen me before."

"No, I can't. The less I see, the less I want, and the less I want, the more comfortable I'll be...physically."

She glanced down and saw the push of his erection against his pants. "Oh."

He draped her baby-doll nightgown around her and the folds fluttered into place. "I'm going to need help with the underpants."

He opened one eye. She held up the emerald-green undies.

"Those are panties, not underpants," Riley said.

Nell frowned. She didn't understand. "What's the difference?"

He shook his head. "Silly girl, underpants are for practicality, panties are for seduction. Trust me, these are seducing me."

"I'm so sorry."

"Wow, no woman has ever asked me to help put her panties *on* before. I don't know the proper procedure."

"I'm sorry," she repeated, looking totally miserable.

"No," he said, "this is good. It's a character-building exercise."

"But—"

Riley interrupted her. "I'm trying to look on the bright side."

How sweet. He was being so understanding, and so compassionate and gentlemanly. Her grandmother used to say men were only after one thing, and here was bad-boy Riley Martin, the object of her grandmother's scorn, proving her wrong. If only the old girl could see him now.

Nell started to giggle. This was the most ludicrous situation she'd ever been in. Her giggle erupted into a belly laugh she couldn't contain. Riley opened one eye and started to grin. His laughter joined her.

He sat on the side of the bed and slapped the bedspread. Finally, he sobered. "What are we laughing at?"

"Many things. That there's a difference between panties and underpants. That you're dressing me instead of undressing me. Three weeks ago I was poor and now I'm not. I'm a virgin and don't want to be. And I'm having absolutely no luck in the sex department."

"And tonight doesn't look any better." He took two pillows and gently propped her foot on top. He fluffed the pillows behind her head. "Are you comfortable? Can I get you something?"

"Almost comfortably numb. A few twinges, but since I can't take the painkillers until tomorrow because of the alcohol I drank at dinner, I think I'm as comfortable as I'm going to get."

She settled back against the pillows, suddenly aware of how truly tired she was. And disappointed. This was supposed to be her big night—the night she had sex for the first time—and here she was laid up with a twisted ankle. Could things get any worse?

Riley stood in the center of the room. He took off his jacket and hung it neatly from a hanger in the closet and then he removed his tie and sat down on the chair to remove his shoes and socks. He reached for the afghan tossed over the foot of the bed and leaned back, arranging the afghan over himself.

"What are you doing?" she asked. He looked ridiculous in that girly chair with its cabbage-rose print.

"I'm sleeping in the chair."

"The bed is plenty big enough." She patted the empty space next to her in the king-size bed.

"No, I'm a roamer at night and I'll hurt your ankle. I'll just sleep here."

Nell frowned at him, disappointed. "Okay." She squirmed down on the bed and pulled the blanket up and tucked it under her arms. "Why did you let me drink so much?"

"Nell, my dear, here lies a life lesson."

"And that life lesson would be?"

"Had I been some random guy and not your caring, devoted friend, I would have plied you with liquor just so I could take advantage of you. A very important rule of thumb when dating—men are dogs. You have to be in control of your behavior, because like dogs, we will exploit any weakness we can find unless, of course, you're a caring, devoted man like me."

Her head spun over that speech. "So what you're saying is men are not to be trusted."

"Not right away. We have to earn that trust."

"Dating is complicated. I have enough money, maybe I'll just buy myself a boy toy."

Riley burst into laughter.

She eyed him with disgust. "Are you laughing at me or with me?"

"I'm a gentleman and a gentleman never tells."

Chapter 11

Nell sat in a corner booth in the diner with her foot propped up on a pillow and paperwork spread out in front of her as she went over her grandmother's estate deciding what she wanted to keep and what she wanted to sell. How had her grandmother dealt with all the mountains of paperwork so easily? When did she have the time? Nell couldn't remember ever seeing her grandmother work at it.

Her grandmother's holdings were much more vast than Nell had realized. She owned property all over the county and had investments that went back thirty years, including stock in Microsoft, which amazed Nell. Her grandmother had invested in high-tech stocks when she'd railed for weeks about having to get rid of her rotary phone and buy some newfangled thing when Wayloo's phone system had been revamped.

Glancing up from the paperwork, Nell could only marvel at her grandmother's shrewdness. Lucy walked up to the table with a pot of coffee in each hand. She poured coffee into Nell's empty cup.

"Mama, I don't drink decaf coffee," Nell said, eyeing the pot with the orange handle to signify the contents were decaf.

Lucy shook her head. "You drink way too much coffee, and if you can't give that up, then you need to switch to decaf at least some of the time."

Nell stared at the full cup of brown liquid. Her stomach roiled at the thought of that swill. She'd give up coffee before she switched. "I don't like decaf."

Lucy patted Nell on the arm. "Oh, darling, trust me on this. Life is a series of compromises. Best to let the little ones slide by and save your fight for the big ones."

Logic was not a trait Nell would have ascribed to her mother. She watched Lucy sashay back to the counter. Had the woman been watching Dr. Phil? She glanced at the TV over the counter, but it was off.

Lucy ran around the restaurant pouring coffee, and Nell marveled at how smoothly Lucy ran her stations. Hell, she ran the whole diner and hardly looked tired. She handled the employees with ease, customers were eating out of her hand and the place ran seamlessly. Nell glanced at the plate of salad greens with a grilled chicken breast on top and marveled. Even the food was better. Nell had noticed little changes around the diner. Health-conscious meals had been added to the menu and there were fewer desserts. Since she hadn't heard any rumblings of discontent, Wayloo seemed to have accepted the changes rather quickly.

Lucy leaned over the counter to flirt with Sheriff Atkins, who seemed to be spending a lot of time at the diner these days. He grinned at her and put a hand over hers. Lucy grinned and blew him a kiss. She didn't want to, but Nell couldn't help but admire her mother.

The door opened and Nell twisted to find Riley entering. He paused and looked around. Spying her, he walked over and slid into the booth next to her.

"Hey, beautiful," he said, affection in his tone as he took her hand in an intimate gesture.

A thrill ran up her spine. His smile sent her pulse into overdrive. And she didn't even want to talk about what his touch was doing to her. "Hi, Riley."

Lucy glanced up from her flirting to wink at Nell. Heat infused her cheeks. *What was that all about?*

"How's the foot?" Riley asked.

"I do love painkillers. I think I found my new best friend." The pain hadn't quite subsided yet, but the ache she felt was distant and controllable. She pushed her paperwork aside.

He leaned over to look at the pile of papers spread across the table. "What are you doing?"

"Just trying to get more paperwork out of the way before I go."

He raised an eyebrow. "Where are you going?"

"I'm leaving for a quick trip to New York for a little fun and relaxation and to visit NYU, Columbia and Fordham campuses for a tour. I'm also going to visit my real estate agent and look at apartments." She was almost wriggling with her excitement. More time away from Wayloo and the sly looks of the men as they attempted to gauge her mood of the moment in hopes she'd be amenable to the next proposal. Her announcement the other day had made absolutely no impression on the men who tracked her down.

"New York?" Riley said, a query in his eyes. Or was that a hint of fear?

"Yes. You want to go with me? It's only few days and I've decided to go for broke and made reservations at the Waldorf-Astoria hotel." She couldn't believe she'd just slipped that one out. She wanted him to say yes, because it would be special to get a taste of the Big Apple with someone who had been such an important part of her life.

He paused to consider her request. "I suppose my crew can take care of things for a few days, and I don't have any business that requires me to be available. You're the only pressing business I have."

He raised his eyebrows and she chuckled. *Please say yes, please say yes, please say yes,* she chanted to herself.

"I don't see why not." He gave her an intimate look. "Seems as though all those lessons you wanted are just not getting done. Too many distractions." He glanced at her mother. "Maybe we should be thousands of miles away from here."

"I may regret this, but I made Chloe swear on a stack of Bibles she would be available if my mother needed her." She held up the cell phone she'd just bought. "Now that I'm connected to the rest of the world with my brand-new cherry-red cell phone, my mother can get in touch with me at any time."

"Nice phone."

"I can take photos, I can do videos and play games. I can probably operate a weather satellite from this phone. My God." She gazed at the phone with affection. "Backwoods Nell Evans is on the cutting edge of technology." She patted the phone. "And I like it."

Riley laughed. "The future of technology—you have embraced the future, grasshopper."

She joined in his laughter and when the laughter died away she said, "Can I ask you a question?"

"Ask away."

Picking up one of the new menus she handed it to him. "As a regular customer of the diner, how do you find things here?"

"With you not being my regular waitress anymore, I think things are a little different and I miss you, but your mom is good at taking care of me. New dishes on the menu, a lot fewer desserts. My favorite coconut-cream marshmallow pie is gone, I'm not real happy about that."

"I think my mother has decided to improve the health of Wayloo—" Nell eyed her coffee "—one customer at a time, whether they want it or not."

"Everyone was a little apprehensive when your mom took your place here in the diner, but Chloe says they're all singing her praises."

Nell glanced at her mother. *That was food for thought, pardon the pun.* The cook in the kitchen called out an order and Lucy started loading up her arms with plates and managed to make it to the customers waiting for their food. She served them all without spilling a drop. Nell hated to admit it, but Lucy was pretty impressive.

"I think my mom is trying to win me over, but I don't know why. I thought it was about the money, but she seems like she couldn't care less. She wants to make peace, but I'm suspicious of her motives and I feel bad because I'm suspicious."

"Nell, you think too much." Riley put his hands flat on the table and leaned forward. "Just go with the flow. Your mom is doing the best she can. Let her do it. People do change." He spread a hand over his chest. "Case in point."

"I know people change, but in my mother's case I'm not sure how I feel." Because her mother had changed, Nell had to look at her in a new way. "I was comfortable with our relationship the way it was."

"You didn't *have* a relationship."

"That's what I mean. Having her home means I have to relate to her in a new way and in some ways I feel a little like my grandmother—waiting for the other shoe to drop." Her mother's wild-child past was beneath the surface just waiting to roll in like a tidal wave. "I'm waiting for her to make a wrong move and justify my grandmother's decision to keep her away from Wayloo." Even though her mother appeared to have turned over a new leaf, Nell was still suspicious. Nell pushed her food aside and leaned her head on the table.

"Let it go, Nell," Riley said. "All this worry and supposition is just wearing you out."

"Maybe you're right." She lifted her head and scrunched up her nose. "I always thought having money would make me happy, but instead it's made me paranoid."

Riley laughed. "Nell, you are so cute when you wrinkle your nose."

Lucy walked over, a coffeepot in each hand. "Riley," she said in her honey-sweet tone, "what can I get you?"

"Sweet tea, a burger—no pickles—and extra sweet potato fries."

"We make unsweetened tea now, Riley," Lucy said, "and maybe you should try one of our new salads instead. We have the fiesta salad with lean ground beef, the Asian chicken salad with nonfat ginger dressing and the Waldorf fruit salad with candied walnuts as a garnish."

Riley looked like a surprised deer caught in the headlights. "But I like burgers."

"All right," Lucy said with a martyred sigh. "I was just trying to keep you healthy and productive." She scribbled his order on her notepad.

"I'm sure Riley appreciates your trying," Nell said.

Lucy hit Riley's arm with her pad. "I'm just thinking about his good health." She walked off, pausing to refill a coffee mug before leaning up against the counter next to Sheriff Atkins.

"What the hell was that?" Riley asked.

"I think she thinks you and I are an item. And that I'll stay in Wayloo so she'll be close to my money." Even as she said it, the words didn't sound quite right, but she couldn't take them back. She hated herself for being so untrusting. That just wasn't who she was, but it was what she seemed to be turning into.

"There you go again, being paranoid."

"See?" Nell said. "See how this money is changing me? It's a burden."

"If you let the money burden you, then it will." He glanced at Lucy still flirting with Sheriff Atkins. "Maybe she wants you to stay in Wayloo for another reason."

"Just what reason would that be?"

"For a smart woman, you can be dense sometimes." Nell frowned. "What do you mean?"

"Didn't you offer your mother money to leave?"

"Yes, but we never settled on a dollar amount."

He palmed his chin. "Are you in negotiation?"

"She turned me down."

"Why do you think she turned you down?" Riley asked.

Nell shrugged. "A little part in the back of my head says she's trying to irritate me so I'll give her more money. But then again, I could be wrong. She wanted us to get to know each other better."

"Why do you think she wants to get to know you better?"

"I have no idea. She never did before."

"Maybe because your grandmother wouldn't allow it."

Nell glanced at her mother who now stood behind the snack counter dishing up a plate of salad for someone who'd obviously agreed to try one. "She's a grown-up who has spent her entire life doing what she wanted whether anyone liked it or not. If she'd wanted to get to know me better, she could have come home more often."

"I can tell you from personal experience, your grandmother could make the Great Wall of China look like a rickety picket fence."

Mentally, Nell conceded to that. "Riley, I don't know. I'm afraid to put my heart out there. As long as Lucy was in another city, I could create any sort of fantasy of what I wanted her to be and nothing could contradict it. Here she is working at the diner and she comes home and fixes me dinner and she's so nice and trying to be understanding. She wants to paint my fingernails. She scares me. Having an attentive mother who's not just a mom but a friend is what I've always dreamed of. But now that she's here I want to hide from her."

"Take what she's offering and see where it goes."

Nell took a deep breath. Maybe he was right. She certainly hadn't come up with a solution, but she was still leery. "That's easy for you to say."

"Yeah! Right! I had the parents from hell."

Aghast, Nell said, "I'm sorry." She knew about his family history. He had a few crazy folks in his family tree. At least her mother went out of town to sow her wild oats so that Nell didn't have a physical reminder.

Nell watched her mother bustling about the diner taking orders, delivering food and ringing up the cash register. For the first time, Nell really looked. Every time Lucy had visited in the past, she'd always had this restless, nervous energy and frown lines, but now she looked content. She was relaxed and Nell noticed she'd put on a couple of pounds. Her model-thin figure had a few curves Nell had never seen before. Her hair, always thick and glossy, had been intricately styled, but now Lucy wore it back in a simple ponytail. This time her beauty was natural. In the past, she'd been perfectly made-up and dressed to the nines. Now she looked ten years younger and happy.

Nell felt a little guilty having such bad thoughts

about her mother. Maybe she *had* changed. Maybe
Nell was letting her resentment get the better of
her. Maybe Nell needed to be the one to do some
soul-searching.

Nell twisted to look at Riley. He'd changed, too.
She remembered one time in high school when his
temper had led him into a huge fight at school. The
fight was justified because Jake John Delacourt,
team quarterback and son of the town banker, had
attacked Riley's younger sister. Riley threw the first
punch and put Wayloo High School's star quarterback out of commission for the season. Everybody
knew the truth of what had happened, and if it had
been a girl from a nice family, Jake John Delacourt
would probably still be doing time. But because
Riley's family had no standing in the community and
no money, Jake John got off with a slap on the wrist.
The only good thing was Jake John losing a full
scholarship at Tulane and a possible football career.
His family had no pull in New Orleans.

So people did change. Nell glanced from Riley to
her mother. Riley was no longer that juvenile delinquent who used to sneak around to the back of the
lockers for a cigarette. And before Nell had inherited
the money, she would never have made that scene
about everyone coming to date her. No…that wasn't
about having money, that was about Riley being in
her life.

The money hadn't changed her as much as Riley
being in her life had. He made her look at herself in

a whole new light. She remembered the few times he had asked her out and not once had he ever been mean when she refused. In fact, he'd gone out of his way to be nice to her. His kindness was one of the qualities about him that she had really liked. And she remembered catching him looking at her. He wasn't judging her, but trying to flirt with her.

Oh, my God, she thought. *How much frickin' time have I wasted?* If she had realized this earlier, her whole life might have been different.

No. No. She wasn't going to think about this. She was leaving Wayloo on her big adventure. This time around, her heart didn't know best. What was she thinking? She'd never listened to her heart before. She'd always listened to her head and she wasn't going to change now.

She swiveled around to study Riley. "Thanks, you've given me a lot to think about."

"You don't sound grateful."

"I will be, just not right now."

Riley dug into his pocket and put some money on the table. "You need a break. Come on." He stood and held out his hand. "Let's go for a ride."

"But your hamburger?"

"Come on. Someone else will eat it." He held her steady as she slid from the booth and picked up her crutches.

"Where are we going?"

"I don't know. Just out of here." He led her toward the door of the diner. He grinned at Lucy who waved. Sheriff Atkins nodded at Riley. Nell felt herself being swept away.

Riley adjusted his seat belt and made certain Nell was settled comfortably with a pillow beneath her foot.

"All set?" he asked

"Good to go," she said. "I'm glad I decided to take more time off from the diner."

He revved the engine and eased out onto the street. In five minutes they were at the edge of town. Riley was glad Wayloo was a one-horse town with little traffic. He might have veered into the wrong lane one too many times. He slowed the big truck down and turned onto a dirt road. He wanted to get as far from civilization as he could.

The road was a little bumpy, but he steered around the worst of the potholes until the old farmhouse came into sight.

"This is a dream come true. I've always wanted to go parking with a cute boy," she said.

"Thanks." He'd taken plenty of girls on this trip, but he didn't think it was any big deal.

"Now, I'm one of the 'in' girls."

"What do you mean?"

"During high school all the girls used to talk about you and your famous trips to the Collier farm. They said taking a ride with you on a country road was like some rite of passage."

"What? Puberty? Your first kiss? Going to the prom? What's the big deal?"

She sighed. "It's a girl thing. The only thing is, I wish we could have taken your motorcycle."

"If you hadn't tripped." He stopped the truck. "Why the motorcycle?"

"For one thing, all the vibration feels kind of nice in all your special spots."

He understood that. Getting that big, vibrating machine between a guy's legs could ease a lot of those special-spot kind of aches. "Oh, really?"

"No matter what, you were always the cutest boy in town."

He parked the truck in front of the barn. "I had no idea of my appeal."

She slanted a wicked glance at him. "Yes, you did. You used that charm and that little-boy smile to get whatever you wanted from any girl."

"If I recall, Miss Nell, my smile and my charm never really worked on you."

"Yes, it did. I was too afraid to act on it."

He helped her out and she stood and looked around, one hand on her hip. "Mr. Collier's farm."

The Colliers hadn't really owned the land for over thirty years, but when a name stuck it stuck. No matter who owned the land, it would always go by the name of Collier. "The Colliers have been gone for years. I don't even know who owns it now." He handed her cane to her.

"I do," she said, using the cane to maneuver around a pile of old lumber. "My grandmother purchased this place about a year ago, which means I own it now."

She leaned heavily on his arm as he led her toward the old farmhouse. He said, "Does that mean we aren't trespassing?"

"I do believe that is the point. Did I just suck all the fun out of this?"

He grinned at her. "Trespassing will never be as much fun as it was during high school."

Nell patted him on the arm. "I have confidence that you will make this a fun outing for me."

He helped her up the steps of the veranda to an old swing that still looked sturdy. She sat down and he was struck by the way the sun lit her face, softening the angular curve of her cheeks. He watched the shadows play across her lips and the way her eyes gazed fondly at him.

He sat down next to her and set the swing into gentle motion. "I've always loved this old house."

The veranda stretched all the way around the house, the overhanging roof supported by white pillars and wrought-iron balustrades. Black shutters framed the floor-to-ceiling windows and inside he could see the house was empty except for a few pieces of dilapidated furniture and cobwebs hanging from the fireplace mantel.

"My grandmother loved it, too. I found a note in her things that suggested she was thinking about hiring you to restore this old place."

"Are you going to sell this place, too, when you move to New York?" he asked.

"I don't know. I know a land developer contacted

her with an offer to purchase both the house and the three hundred acres attached to it."

"You would let someone tear down this old house?" His heart clenched.

"Honestly, Riley, I don't know. Look how bad it's gotten with an absentee landlord."

Riley saw the weeds in the field and felt the slight give of the planks under his feet. Even though the house had been built in the 1850s it was still solid. It might need a lot of cosmetic work and probably some interior support work, but it would be worth trying to fix it up. "I think this old girl would be worth restoring."

Nell glanced around. "I don't know. The house is probably filled with beer bottles and used condoms. I'm sure a lot of the local wildlife has made itself at home."

"What do you know about beer bottles and used condoms?"

"I may be a virgin," she said with a slight laugh, "but I'm not an idiot. I read. I go to movies. I have cable."

"I'll bet you just got cable in the last couple of weeks."

She grinned. "Guilty as charged. I'm not ashamed to say, I bought air-conditioning and cable two days after the will was read."

Riley burst out laughing. "You are living high on the hog now, aren't you?"

She shrugged. "My grandmother lived frugally, as

if we didn't have a nickel. I like having a few luxuries, but I'm not going crazy. It's a good thing her house came with indoor plumbing when she bought it, because she would never have had it installed."

Holding in his chuckle, he could just see Nell tripping to the outhouse in the middle of the night complaining the entire way.

The porch swing moved gently beneath them. A tiny squeak made itself known with every motion. Which didn't seem to bother her one bit. Nell leaned against him, her eyes half-closed. The heat of her body against his reminded him of their lessons in love. But just having her so close was enough to cause his heart rate to rise.

He leaned his chin against her hair and found himself soothed by the rhythm of the swing. Birds darted across the overgrown lawn. A late-summer butterfly flitted across a tangle of wild flowers. Billowy clouds drifted overhead that reminded him of childhood and how he used to create shapes out of them. A bee buzzed around them, but then left. A bird landed on the top step, but, startled by the squeak of the swing, took off again.

Riley wanted this moment to go on and on. He imagined all the things he would do to restore the house. He'd visited the house a month before Miz Sarah had died, with the idea of purchasing it. At the time he'd had no idea Miz Sarah owned it. He'd been dreaming then as he was dreaming now. He closed his eyes and in his imagination he saw Nell in a long flowing dress walking through the garden, a basket of flowers over her arm and a floppy-brimmed hat in one hand while a gentle breeze caught at the strands of her hair.

He drifted into a hazy half sleep, his arms firmly around Nell, her back tucked against his side with her sprained ankle resting up on the bench. He felt the rise and fall of her breasts against his arms and the faint flutter of her breath on his skin.

Never had he felt so at peace, so contented. Nell stirred in his arms, and he glanced down. She'd fallen asleep and her face was so relaxed and so beautiful. He slid her hand into his and stroked her long fingers. Her hands were solid and strong, yet delicate. He imagined them on his skin, stroking and lighting fires that would never again be extinguished.

A stirring deep inside him reminded him of all the years he'd repressed his feelings for her, all the years he'd stayed away because her grandmother had disapproved of him.

What would life have been like if he'd defied Miz Sarah and taken Nell out and made love to her if he could have created the opportunity? That was so much water under the bridge. Now, he was no longer the man for her. She needed a man who could love her with his entire heart. And his was just too broken. Her leaving for New York was a good thing. If she stayed, he might destroy her because he wasn't

capable of being the man she needed. Everything
that was right inside him had become closed with
Benjy's death. He'd chased Chloe away and she
cared for him.

Chloe had told him that he couldn't let go of his
grief because he believed if he did, he would lose
his love for Benjy. As Riley swung back and forth
lazily with Nell in his arms, he knew she was right.
He couldn't let go because he couldn't risk losing
all the wonderful memories of Benjy's life. Like
the first step he'd taken. The first words he'd said.
The first time he'd caught a baseball. His first
soccer game. The time Riley had taken Benjy for
a ride on his Harley and how Benjy had laughed
with such excitement he could barely keep his
hold. These were the personal memories he and
Benjy had shared.

Riley had so looked forward to sharing with
Benjy all the things fathers and sons were supposed
to do: camping, fishing, fixing cars and building dog
houses. Chloe had once asked him what if Benjy
didn't like to fish or camp and Riley had replied he
would do what Benjy wanted. If he'd wanted to play
the cello instead of baseball, Riley would have been
happy as long as Benjy had been happy.

He felt an unaccustomed tickle of tears at the
corners of his eyes. He brushed them away. He'd
refused to cry then and he wouldn't cry now.
Nothing mattered about what Benjy did, Riley had
just wanted to be there for him, to share, to experi-

ence, to love. And now everything was gone, nothing was left except his pain.

Nell stirred in his arms. He couldn't share his pain with her. He didn't want to burden her. If he were a kind, compassionate man, he'd kick her to the curb right now, but some part of him just wanted to play a little role in her great adventure.

Chapter 12

Riley sat next to Nell in the cab. Nell leaned forward, her hands pressed to the glass. "Oh, my God," she whispered, looking up.

Riley hid a smile. He'd been to New York often enough to know he didn't want to live there. The city was too big, too crowded and too dirty for him. But he could understand Nell's fascination.

The taxi driver grinned at Nell's whispers. He'd given them a small tour of the city and now they were cruising down Park Avenue. Nell craned her neck to look up at the towering buildings. She was like a kid at the circus, her mouth open in awe and her face alight with wonder.

"I want to visit the Statue of Liberty," Nell said

as the taxi stopped at a light and a crowd of people surged into the crosswalk. "And I want to see the Empire State Building and Times Square and Central Park. And would it be in bad taste if I want to see Ground Zero?"

"It's the number-one site for all the visitors, miss," the cab driver said from the front seat.

The light turned green.

A man still in the crosswalk picked up his pace. A taxi jumped forward and almost hit the man. He slapped his hand on the hood of the taxi. The driver leaned out to scream invectives at him in a foreign language and give him the one-finger salute. The man saluted back with his own cursing.

"Nell," Riley said, keeping his laughter in check, "you are not driving in this city. New York is not Wayloo. Hell, this is worse than the Daytona 500."

Nell watched as the taxi sprinted forward, the driver still hanging half out the window cursing at the pedestrian. Nell's mouth fell open in astonishment. She didn't know cursing could be so inventive. "People are really rude here."

"Rule number one: New York is all about survival of the fittest."

She gulped, but didn't stop staring.

A few minutes later the taxi turned smoothly into the passenger drop-off in front of the hotel. A bellman opened the door and Nell slid out, staring around her. Her mouth opened and closed and she made small choking sounds. Riley took her hand

and led her inside. "Honey, if you keep staring they won't let you in."

He hated to admit it to himself, but even he was a little awed as they stepped into the lobby, with its art deco theme: marble floors and massive crystal chandeliers. He'd never been inside the Waldorf before and he felt a sudden sense of what Nell was feeling.

The bellman directed them to the check-in desk.

A few seconds later, he found himself smiling at a uniformed woman who registered them and watched as Nell stared at the key card the woman handed to her.

"Your luggage will be brought up shortly," the woman assured Nell.

Nell nodded without speaking. She gripped the card in both hands.

Riley thanked the woman and took Nell's hand, leading her toward the elevator, wondering if he was ever going to get the card away from her.

"Oh, my," Nell cried when she stepped into their suite. "This isn't real." She walked around the living room and suddenly plopped down into an overstuffed chair. Her skirt flared and Riley saw a bit of leg and for a second the world tilted on its axis. "This is so elegant. Everything is so classy. I want to live here forever."

As an historical restorationist, Riley had seen some lavish homes, but this room was unabashed hedonistic luxury. His eyes narrowed as he took in every little detail from the opulent fabrics to the ankle-deep pile carpet. He was impressed with the attention to detail and he never knew when he would need to pull out the knowledge for a project.

Nell bounced up and down on the chair. "Riley, this is the most comfortable chair I've ever sat in. I wonder where I can buy a chair like this. Wait, wait," she sighed. "That's just a pipe dream. I have to be careful or I'll spend everything in a year. This trip is the last extravagance I'll have for a long time."

"Nell, stop being so strict with yourself," Riley said as he sat on the sofa watching her. "Not too many people deserve to live a little more extravagantly than you do. So just relax and enjoy."

She ran her fingers down the nap of the fabric. "I think I'm gonna cry. This is so exciting."

Riley held his arms out to her and she sat down and let him cuddle her. "You have every right to be excited. You've done a lot of firsts today. Your first plane flight. Your first taxi ride. Your first glimpse of New York City. Just savor the moment and enjoy."

"I want to ride the subway." She curled in next to Riley and closed her eyes. "I want to take a cruise on the Staten Island Ferry."

He'd done it one time to visit a college buddy and that was enough for him. "I've been on the ferry. It's just a big boat and not a whole lot of fun."

"Okay, fine. I'm taking a chance here, but I would love a ride around Central Park in a carriage."

"What the hell, let's live dangerously. I'm game."

She pulled out her spiral notebook and flipped it open. "Broadway shows. Check."

"What are we seeing?"

She opened a narrow envelope. "*A Chorus Line, Phantom of the Opera* and *The Lion King.*"

He wasn't surprised she wanted to go to a play, but he'd figured she'd want to go see something new. "You have all the movies on tape. Why don't you see something new?"

"I spent a lot of money on the tickets and I know I already like them." Nell turned to him. "Are you politely trying to say I should have asked what you wanted to see?"

Cute, practical Nell. He hoped that would never change about her. "You've spent a lot of money for this trip. You could pick whatever you wanted to see."

"I want you to have a good time, too. You know I have money to get anything I want last minute."

He held up his hand. "You've spent enough money for this trip. And we've had this go-round before. At least allow me to buy our meals."

"All right."

The mutinous expression on her face told him he needed to make certain she wasn't going to drag him to every cheap place to eat. "And we are not going fast food. We are going to eat in restaurants with cloth napkins and a wine steward."

"How do we find a good restaurant?"

Riley hugged her. She was too sweet. "Trust me.

I've been here before and I know where we're going
first." He reached for his cell phone.

Nell could hardly stay still. Excitement tickled
every nerve ending in her body. She walked down
Park Avenue with her hand tucked firmly in Riley's
and felt as though she would never see enough. The
buildings towered over her. The traffic was so heavy
the exhaust fumes almost made her dizzy. The noise,
the traffic, the people made her feel alive in a way
she'd never been before. She felt as though her
whole life in Wayloo existed on another planet.

"I can't believe I'm finally here," she said.

"This is your big adventure."

"Yes." She grasped her cane and gave a little jump
that didn't stress her ankle. "I'm so excited. Every
morning I wake up and can hardly wait to start my
day. I've never felt this way before." Remembering
that her new life had come because of her grandmother's sacrifices made her pause, but she started
skipping again, unable to keep everything inside her
contained. "I'm going to burst."

"You'll make a mess on the sidewalk," Riley
warned.

She stopped and stared at him a second before
seeing the amusement in his eyes. "You're kidding
me."

"I can't help it." He burst out laughing. "You are
so much fun, Nell. I've never been with someone who
sees things the way you do. Promise me something."

"What?"

"That you will never lose that sense of wonder."

"I don't think that will ever happen. I think I could live in New York for twenty years and never feel jaded."

Riley squeezed her hand. "I hope so."

They window-shopped for a bit. She couldn't wait to go to Macy's or Sak's Fifth Avenue. All the stores she'd ever dreamed of were right here at her fingertips. "I know I don't have any children, but I want to go to FAO Schwarz. I've read the ice cream is fabulous. And the toys." She used to dream about the toys at FAO Schwarz. The Internet had a Web site and she'd bookmarked it because she so enjoyed looking at the toys.

"Nell, you're going to live here, and will have a lot of time to visit all these places. You don't have to pack it all in today or tomorrow."

"But you're with me now and I want to do some of these things with you. When I move here, I won't have any friends and I'll have to sightsee all alone." She gripped his hand tightly. A woman wearing a business suit and jogging shoes sprinted past them, brushing against Nell. Nell stumbled as she watched the woman burst into a run and hail a bus just about to close its doors. The bus waited a half second and the woman jumped on board.

The air had a crisp, autumn feel to it. A few trees in a tiny park squeezed in between two tall buildings had already turned to their fall colors.

"Where are we heading?" she asked as he stepped to the curb and hailed a cab.

"We are going to see one of the jewels in the crown of New York City."

A taxi screeched to a stop and Riley opened the door and helped Nell inside, positioning her ankle as comfortably as possible, then running around the other side of the cab and getting in.

She settled her cane against her leg. "One of the crown jewels?" she asked curiously, urging him to continue.

Riley settled himself next to her and told the driver, "Radio City Music Hall." He turned to Nell and said, "Rockefeller Center, Saint Patrick's Cathedral and, if you'd like, Sak's Fifth Avenue."

"Music, commerce, religion and shopping. Nothing could be better than this." She almost pinched herself, thinking about all the things she could do.

She watched the passersby, the traffic, the tall buildings that flanked her as the taxi roared down the street. She could barely breathe. She had so much to catch up on. So much to do. And so little time.

They approached with Radio City Music Hall on their right and the Rockefeller Center on the left. Nell tingled with excitement. The taxi stopped. Riley paid the driver and helped Nell out. She stood on the sidewalk to study a lighted sign. "Maybe we can take in a concert here? What kind of music do you like?"

"I'm more into jazz and the blues. What do you like?" He took her hand.

She leaned heavily on her cane. "Look, the tickets are available."

"I don't want to be the rain cloud on your parade, but…"

She held up a hand. "You're going to try and talk sense into me, aren't you."

"No, I want you to go out and live your life, and find that pot of gold at the end of the rainbow. But for heaven's sake, don't rush into anything. Employ a bit of caution. There is nothing wrong…"

"Stop." She held a hand over her ear for a second and then stamped her good foot. "I don't need a life lesson."

"I'm worried about you."

Nell smiled, trying to reassure him she could take care of herself so far from home. "I understand New York City isn't Wayloo. I'll have to lock my doors and I won't be able to talk to every stranger on the street, and as soon as my cast is off, I'm starting my self-defense class." Though her ankle didn't hurt anymore the doctor had asked her to wear the walking cast for another couple of weeks just to protect her foot.

"Good. Self-defense is a good skill to have." He took her hand and they started walking. The crowds parted around them and Nell had to be careful with her cane.

"Every place I'm going to be looking at with the real estate agent has a doorman and high-tech security systems. I'm going to be just fine. And since I don't have to work and I won't be at school every day, I'm getting myself a very big dog."

"What kind of dog?"

"I'm thinking about a German shepherd, an Akita, Rottweiler or a Doberman pinscher. But to be honest, I really like the look of the Rhodesian ridgeback. They're African, you know."

"Good. When you said 'big dog,' I pictured an English sheepdog or something else with a cute face and floppy ears."

"Nope. I'm getting a dog that says in big, bold letters, 'Don't mess with me.' But since my dog will only be a puppy, no one is going to say that for a few months."

"Good," Riley said, approval in his voice. "You're doing all the right things for a woman alone in a big city. Remember, you can't go out with every man who asks you."

"I know that. I spent the last three weeks realizing that fact." Laughter bubbled up inside her at the memory of all the men in Wayloo putting on their Sunday best to woo her and her money.

"I need you to promise me something," Riley said. "Never let them pick you up for the first date. Meet them somewhere public."

"I know. I read that in the *Single Girl's Survival Guide to the Big City*. I ordered the book off the Internet. It's been pretty helpful."

"Do you study everything in such depth?"

"When I want something bad enough I do. I was a pretty good student when we were still in school. I've been planning my escape to New York City since I was ten. I always thought it was a pipe dream, but now, it's just fallen into my lap, and I refuse to screw it up."

"I'm glad you have a game plan," Riley said.

Her own tenaciousness surprised even her, but she was okay with it. "A quarter of my life is over and it's been pretty damn dull." More than dull—claustrophobic.

"Do you think you've wasted your life?"

She tilted her head up to him. "Not wasted, just not moving forward as much as I would like. I've always known my grandmother wouldn't live forever and I've always had all these fanciful thoughts in the back of my mind. I've always asked myself what I would do after Grandma passed. I did have some options. I knew I'd inherit the diner and could spend the rest of my life working there. I'd have a place to live." She paused as she thought her way through all the ideas in her head. "But I would have been alone, and I didn't want to be alone."

Riley and all her school friends had long since married and started families. For a long time, she'd been outside the windows of their lives looking in and seeing their happiness and contentment. The life she wanted was never going to happen for her unless she left Wayloo.

Though fate had brought Riley back into her life, she had never allowed herself to dream of a future with him. Fate had changed her, too. Instead of struggling through her dream, now she had the opportunity to do what she wanted, and nothing was going to stop her. "Don't get me wrong, and please don't think poorly of me, but I get to do all this in style. I can shop where I want, I can buy tickets to Broadway shows, I can travel to Europe or Africa. I can do whatever I want." She could be her own person. Make her own decisions. Do what she wanted. "I think I'm going to appreciate my life more now than I ever would have at eighteen."

She stared up at the marquee for Radio City Music Hall. The lights, the colors, the ideas inside the building represented everything she had ever dreamed about, but never quite dared to want. And now she was here, finally here, ready to start the next chapter of her life.

"I had no idea you had so much trapped behind your calm, sweet, naive facade."

"I'm a woman of great passion."

He smiled at her and squeezed her hand. "Yes, you are and we're going to uncork some of that this week."

She looked away, embarrassed at her thoughts of Riley and the feel of him stretched out next to her on the bed. She had never thought that losing her virginity would turn into such a big production. When she'd envisioned asking Riley for help, she had thought they would kiss and he would woo her a little bit and then they'd jump into bed. When had her plan gotten so complicated? Not that the complications hadn't been fun, but she was torn. She liked the complications, but didn't want to deal with them. So much about her life was simple and easy. She'd made all her arrangements for her move over the Internet. No muss, no fuss, point and click and call it a day.

But what she had going on with Riley wasn't so cut-and-dried. She'd always liked him as a person, but she'd had no idea how deep and complex he was, and even worse than that, how much she had come to like that about him.

With Riley, she didn't feel as if she had to be good-girl Nell. She didn't have to be polite, or say the right things, or be above reproach. If she wanted to cuss, she cussed. She felt liberated being with him.

He led her toward Rockefeller Center. A row of antique cars, surrounded by people, lined the center of the plaza.

"Getting hungry yet?" Riley asked as they strolled down the line of antique cars.

"After my tirade? Yes, I am."

"That wasn't a tirade," he said. "You were telling me how you felt and there isn't anything wrong with that. You haven't done much in your life and you have a lot of time to catch up. You know what you want, Nell, and I have to say, you're not going to fall for anything." He led the way toward a restaurant. "If things don't work out, you can always come back home."

"But would I want to? Nothing is there anymore for me."

A look crossed over his face. "Are you really sure nothing is left in Wayloo for you?"

She sensed something more meaningful in his tone, but as she studied his face, she saw nothing but the Riley she knew. "I have to be or else I'll never leave." Never find her future anything.

Riley spoke to the hostess, who smiled at them politely. "Do you have a reservation?"

"Yes, I called earlier." Riley gave his name. "I know we're a little early."

"Not a problem," the hostess said with a gracious smile. She consulted the reservations list in front of her and then stepped out from behind the desk. "Please come with me."

Nell followed the hostess to a table overlooking the skating rink. But instead of a skating rink, it was an outdoor restaurant. She made a mental promise to come here during the winter so she could see the ice-skaters.

After they were seated their waitress took their drink order. Nell ordered a martini.

"Do you have a preference, madam?" the waitress asked politely.

"What kind of martinis do you have?"

"Apple, mango, peach, pear, chocolate…"

"I want to try all of them." Nell clapped her hands together, excited to try her first martini.

The waitress's eyebrows rose. "At one time?"

"You can't have all those," Riley said. "Remember what happened in New Orleans?"

"I know," she said with a sigh. "I just think they all sound so good."

"Why don't you try a mango," Riley suggested, "and if you don't like it, you can try something else." He ordered a Scotch on the rocks and Nell thought he looked faintly worried. He leaned forward across the table. "You don't have to drink to prove that you fit in."

Nell glanced around at the other diners. They all looked so sophisticated and elegant. Among them she felt like a country cousin. "A part of me is worried about looking like a country bumpkin."

"Nell, you're a girl from a small town and that's nothing to be ashamed of."

"I'm not ashamed of coming from a small town. I'm afraid of being unsophisticated and not fitting in."

Riley twined his fingers around her hand. "You'll learn what you need to know, but don't let the big city kill the small-town heart. That heart is what makes you special."

She sighed. She didn't think her small-town background made her special, but his words made her feel better. Their drinks came and the waitress hovered a moment while Nell took a sip. She nodded and the waitress disappeared back toward the kitchen. "You always know the right thing to say to me, Riley."

"Yeah, well, if I were smarter I'd figure out how to keep you safely home in Wayloo."

"I'm so tired of being safe," she said, then took a sip. The sweet fruity taste of the fruit and the slight burn of the vodka rolled over her tongue. The mango martini was really good. She sipped it slowly, savoring the sweetness.

"What's wrong with being safe?"

How did she explain this to the once-infamous bad boy. "When a person plays it safe, she ends up a twenty-five-year-old virgin living in her grandmother's house not knowing what goes on in the real world and getting dreams out of books and magazines instead of living them."

Again, that odd look passed over Riley's face and was quickly gone. "But, Nell…"

"You left Wayloo and never looked back."

"No, I just *came* back." He looked sad. "If you are absolutely certain this is what you want, then I'll do everything I can to make it happen for you."

How could she tell him he'd done so much for her already? "You're doing the big part by giving me some big-city polish."

"I know. What else do you have planned while you're here?"

She pulled her notebook out of her purse and flipped it open. The notebook was getting dog-eared and just plain worn-out. Her list was two pages long, but she knew she wouldn't get everything done at once. "I think I have to buy myself a PDA. This old notebook is really falling apart." But once she bought the PDA she would have to learn how to use it. How hard could that be? She used a computer and understood that. Wasn't a PDA just a smaller version of a computer? She would have to research that, and she made a small note to herself on a blank page in her notebook.

"Okay," she said, returning to her list. "Number one is to check out NYU, Fordham and Columbia."

"Have you been accepted?"

"Not yet, but I let the admissions offices know I could pay my tuition up front. I'm sure that will be in my favor."

Riley laughed. "Money does talk."

"And mine is going to talk me into a college degree. With a lot of hard work of course." She read the next item on her long list. "I have an appointment tomorrow with the real estate agent who has seven or eight properties around the city for me to look at."

"Are you buying or renting?"

"Right now, I'm renting. I don't see a need to buy just yet. And I want to do the tourist thing. I can mark Rockefeller Center off my list. And I want to see Times Square which we'll see tomorrow anyway because we have tickets to *Phantom* for tomorrow night. I want to take a tour on those cute little double-decker buses." She reached the last item on her list—lose my virginity—and she felt heat start at the base of her neck and work its way up her cheeks. Okay, she wasn't going to mention that one again, since this particular item had already carried over from several previous lists.

"We can do all that."

She realized she'd filled up all their time in New

York with her list, but what about Riley? "I'm being selfish. Is there anything you want to see?"

He thought for a second. "I've been to New York several times and have everything covered."

"Boy, talk about sounding jaded."

He chuckled. "Okay, I love the Guggenheim Museum."

"I have the Guggenheim on my list for something to do after I move here. If I want to contemplate a painting all day, I don't want to feel in a rush to do so."

A look of disappointment filled his eyes.

"But," she said quickly, "if you want to visit the Guggenheim, we can do that. Who knows, I just might fall in love with the first apartment I see and have to have it."

"Nell, this isn't about pleasing me, but about pleasing you. You can be selfish. No, I wouldn't call you selfish."

"But I want you to have a good time, too."

He grinned. "I'm having a wonderful time."

She turned his statement over in her mind, trying to decide if he was telling her the truth. "Okay, we'll put the museum on hold as a backup in case something else falls through."

The waitress came for their order. They fell quiet for a while. Nell sipped her martini and watched the diners outside the window.

Riley looked lost in his own thoughts. The next time she came to this restaurant for lunch, she could watch the skaters. She could take ice-skating lessons. She'd always wanted to ice-skate, but the only ice in Wayloo came out of the freezer. Everything was going perfectly as planned. All her dreams were falling into place and she finally had the opportunity to start her life. As she watched the other diners, she knew she'd made the right decision.

Chapter 13

Riley's nerves fluttered as though he were sixteen again. Before Nell disappeared into the bathroom with her nightgown over her arm, she tossed him a saucy wink over her shoulder. All the blood rushed out of his head. The door closed and Riley almost jumped out of his clothes and into bed before she returned. He made himself slow down, fold his clothes neatly and hang up his pants and jacket.

He flung the blankets back and climbed into the bed. The sheets were so luxurious and rich in texture he couldn't help running his hands over the smooth fabric. This was how seduction should be.

From the bathroom, Nell was singing. She didn't have a half-bad voice, though she cracked on the high notes. Her tone was seductive and made his heart beat wildly.

The door opened and Nell reappeared, dressed in a tiny black nightgown, the hem barely skimming the tops of her thighs. A small triangle of lace covered the apex of her legs, and her breasts seemed barely contained by the tiny scraps of fabric covering them.

His whole body quivered with desire for her, but the one part of him that was stiffly at attention was ready for finesse.

"Come to bed, Nell," Riley said, patting the empty spot next to him in the king-size bed.

She moved slowly across the room with only a trace of the limp from her hurt ankle. She slid into bed, the thin fabric of her nightgown pulling tightly over her breasts as she wriggled her hips to slide across the sheet. Her breasts bounced and Riley grew harder. He reached for her and she slid into his arms and pressed tightly against him. He slid a finger over her pebbled nipple and she snuggled against him.

He drew her down to lie next to him.

"This bed is the most comfortable bed in the world," she said as she wriggled down, brushing against him. "Did you know you can buy this bed? I think I'm going to buy this bed. I mean, not this particular bed, but one just like it. The hotel sells the mattresses on their Web site along with the sheets. When I move into my apartment, I'm going to decorate just like this. But I don't think I want the sheets, because I want something with a little more color. Grandma was always partial to white sheets. Boring. Boring. Boring. I think I'll get some in fire engine-red."

Her voice rattled on and Riley could only smile. She was nervous, he could tell.

He ran his fingers across her taut nipples. She shivered in his arms. "Nell—"

But she just kept on going and going. "I can buy bath products, a teapot, cookbooks. I can practically furnish my entire life through the Waldorf-Astoria hotel. That is…just so…simple and easy." Her voice ended on a breathless note as Riley's hands moved down the slope of her breasts to her stomach and then lower still.

"Nell," he said.

"What?" She wriggled against his erection and he almost groaned.

"Are you nervous?"

"No way!" She gave a high-pitched laugh. "Why would I be nervous?"

His fingers slid farther down and when he touched that most intimate part of her she jumped. He jerked his hand back. "Nell, I think I'm going to take a shower and give you time to calm down." He didn't want to frighten her. He wanted to make this night special for her. More than special, something memorable she'd have for the rest of her life. The way it would be for him.

"I am calm," she said in her breathless little gasping voice.

He slipped out of bed and walked to the bathroom, painfully aware of the head of his penis against the fabric of his boxers. Part of him wanted to hide his erection, but that would be ridiculous. He heard Nell sigh and he wondered if she was relieved he'd backed off. She wasn't ready yet, but he was good to go.

He turned the water on as cold as he could, stripped off his boxers and stepped inside the marble shower. Water cascaded down his skin and he leaned against the wall waiting for his control to return.

Nell was too delectable, too wonderful. He wasn't going to be a sixty-second man for her. She deserved the best he could give her. He'd been waiting so many years for this, he couldn't screw up now.

He soaped off his skin, avoiding the one place his hands could do the most good and after a few more minutes, the throb in his groin subsided a bit.

As much as he wanted Nell, he was afraid to touch her. He knew tonight was going to be the best he could give her. He didn't want to frighten her so much she couldn't relax and enjoy herself.

Tonight was for her pleasure. He didn't have what she needed inside him anymore; he was an empty man, a shell, with nothing but his grief and his memories. Knowing he wasn't the man she wanted would make letting her go easier.

He rinsed off and stepped outside the shower, wrapping the thick towel around him. Even he was impressed with the luxury of the Waldorf-Astoria and he'd stayed in some pretty luxurious hotels during his own travels. He dried off and pulled his boxers back on. He walked back into the bedroom and stood for a moment watching Nell.

She lay on the bed, propped up against the pillow, yawning. She squinted at him. "You look really sexy in those boxers." She yawned again.

"You look really tired."

"I took a pain pill."

"You took a pain pill after the wine and the martini you drank?" He sat down on the edge of the mattress. "That wasn't very smart, Nell." He glanced at his watch. He'd give her about ten minutes before she would be out for the count.

She rested against the pillow with her hand over her head. She reminded him of a poster of one of those old-time screen sirens. "My ankle really started hurting. And I only took half a one."

He took her hand in his and leaned over to kiss her on the forehead. "Nell, go to sleep."

Her hand reached out to him. "Will you hold me for a while? Please."

"Anything you want, baby." He walked around and climbed into the bed. She snuggled up against him and his erection started throbbing again. He could do this, hold her and let her go to sleep.

She relaxed in his arms. One breast had fallen out of the fabric that had cupped it and her nipple was peaked and full. He wanted so much to touch her, to cup her breasts, to make her feel the sweetness of all that sex could be.

Her breathing quieted and she relaxed against him. He half smiled as he rested against the mound of pillows behind him. Cradled in the pillows, his arms around Nell, he let himself slide into a half sleep. At some point, he reached over and turned out the light. Though the room was almost dark, a sliver of light showed through the drapes outlining her sweet face.

As the night moved on, he memorized the lines of her face, the slope of her cheeks and the fullness of her mouth. At some point, he fell asleep.

Riley walked around the small apartment studying the leaking faucet on the kitchenette sink, the chipped enamel and the worn countertops. The rental agent, a brittle-looking woman who was too thin and too blond, pointed out an architectural detail on the ceiling while Nell simply looked around. Nell didn't look impressed, but she wasn't running away screaming. Maybe that was a good thing.

The agent was beginning to lose her perkiness at Nell's reluctance. "This is a great apartment in a nice area, and you do have a doorman for safety. The plumbing and electrical were all redone in the last three years. Any improvements you want to make are negotiable. They allow dogs with no size limit and you're three blocks from a dog park. The subway is a block away and you're only ten minutes from Manhattan. You won't find anything of this quality for this price anywhere else."

"I like the hardwood floors." Nell tapped her finger on her chin.

The apartment was certainly large enough, Riley mused. Two medium-sized bedrooms, a large living room and kitchenette with nine-foot ceilings. Only two closets, but one was a walk-in. The bathroom was a little small, but then Riley was all about his comfort. And the claw-foot tub was big enough for two. The hardwood floors were in okay condition, though they squeaked. Nell frowned as she looked at the ceiling, which showed a little water damage. Riley joined her at the window. She glanced down at the street.

"This place is going to be hot in the summer. No cross-ventilation," Riley said. And judging by the ancient look of the air conditioner, it would have to be replaced. "Why not one of the apartments in Manhattan?"

Nell frowned. "I'm not paying all that money for five hundred square feet of nothing."

"You can afford it."

"I may have money but I don't think I'll ever know how to be rich. And after a day and a half in New York, I've discovered living isn't cheap. This apartment is nice and it's safe." She tapped the window overlooking the tree-lined street. "I like this neighborhood. So what if the floor is creaky and I'll have to replace the air-conditioning? A month after I move in, I'll know everyone's first name and we'll be meeting for coffee on the weekends."

She was right. He could fix the problems in a weekend and she'd be comfortable for years. This was his own madness. He didn't want her to go, and he was looking for ways to prevent her leaving. He was being selfish and felt a little guilty for it. He'd had his adventure and the memories left behind were good ones. Though he and Chloe had not had a place this nice when they'd first moved, they'd been happy enough with Benjy on the way and his offer of a decent job. Hell, they'd barely been able to afford a cardboard box.

"Okay," Nell said, turning to the rental agent. "Where do I sign?"

Riley felt shock course through him. "But you haven't set a moving date."

"The expense to keep the apartment is minimal. I would rather have this settled than unsettled." Nell smiled as she looked around.

Riley's heart sank to his feet. Nell had become something really important in his life and he didn't know if he could let her go. All his life he'd wanted her and now that he had her, it was only on a temporary basis.

Her expressive face showed her excitement. She was so happy to be doing what she wanted, and she was going to move on with her life without him.

He had not been so excited about his days for a long time until Nell had asked him to help her. He didn't want to lose that feeling.

"Riley," Nell said. "Is something wrong?"

"No, I was just thinking about finding the time to fix all these things."

She shook the ballpoint pen at him. "You don't have to come back here. I'm sure I can find someone handy with a hammer in Brooklyn."

"I'm not going to charge you an arm, a leg and a kidney to do it. And I'll do the job right the first time." Those were his words, but in his head he was trying to find a way to keep her in his life even if he had to come to New York to do it.

"You are so sweet, Riley, but isn't that something I can talk to my landlord about?"

"Well, I guess. But I don't mind doing it." *Yeah! Sweet! That's me.* He'd gone from being the bad boy in town to being sweet! He wanted to keep on being the bad boy. Women don't walk out on bad boys. Bad boys walk out on them and they don't get broken hearts. Nor did they look back or have any regrets. But he was going to let Nell go because he had to. All he hoped was that she didn't push him out of her life.

He looked down at the tree-lined street. Cars hugged the curbs. A couple of boys walked down the street with backpacks. A young couple strolled past, the man pushing a stroller. A woman with grocery bags walked up the steps of the apartment complex across the street. This was a family neighborhood and Nell would fit in here. She could still be a small-town girl with a little big-city polish that would make her more interesting. He was sorry he would never get to know that woman.

He glanced at Nell talking to the rental agent.

"I'll have the paperwork delivered to your hotel in the morning," the agent purred, knowing a good deal when she saw one.

Nell only nodded. She walked around the large empty space with a look on her face Riley recognized. He could see she was already calculating what she was going to do and as her gaze darted around the room, he imagined her placing the sofa against one of the walls and filling it in with two chairs and maybe a rug. He remembered when he and Chloe had finally had enough money to furnish their own apartment. Chloe had dragged him and Benjy around the whole city to every furniture sale, to every department store for sheets and blankets. Yeah, Nell was feeling her decorating zen.

He knew that look on Nell's face because it was a duplicate of the one on Chloe's face when she'd finally figured out she could actually do what she wanted to do after all the time of dreaming.

The curtain fell on the final act of *Phantom of the Opera*. Nell wiped at the tears on her face. Oh! To be loved like that. She glanced at Riley who had a bemused look on his face. A little part of her had always been in love with him, but she had never dared to think he could love her. And here they were, both single and all grown up and the past was behind them. Unfortunately, he couldn't love again. She understood that a part of him had died with his son. But she was determined to be happy with what he could give her.

In the back of her mind though, a niggling little thought told her she was settling for what he could give and she was going to be happy.

The applause finally died away. The lights went on. She took Riley's hand as they entered the aisle with all the other playgoers streaming up to the doors.

Outside, the street was lit up with neon lights.

"So, how do you feel about your first Broadway show?"

She felt drunk, alive, invigorated. "The show was everything I dreamed it would be."

"You dreamed about the *Phantom?*"

She laughed, staring up at the marquee sign. "I would have been happy to see *Seussical.*"

"Once you're living here you can go see a show whenever you want. But you'll have to go alone."

"Only if I want to. On the Internet I found this group of people who get together and go to Broadway shows. I'm seriously thinking about joining. We would all have at least one interest to share."

"You have to be careful of people you meet over the Internet."

"Riley, I know all that," she said as they stood in line waiting for a taxi. "Yes, I'm from a small town. Yes, I'm naive, but I'm still a fairly smart woman. You keep harping on this."

"I… I…care about you, Nell," he finally stuttered, his hand gripping hers tightly.

That must have been hard to say, she thought. "I appreciate your concern. I really do. I'm prepared.

I've done my research. And if I make mistakes, at least I'm making them in the life *I* choose."

The line moved forward as the taxis shot out onto the street.

"When you were in Chicago, who did all the worrying about your social life, or if you were safe or where to buy toilet paper?" she asked.

"I'm a man."

She rolled her eyes at his just-sucked-a-lemon expression. "Fine, what about Chloe?"

"She had me to take care of her."

"You sound worse than an old woman," Nell said. She had wanted to say *father,* but stopped herself.

He looked annoyed. "I resent that."

"Go ahead. You still sound like an old woman worrying about her offspring out on some junket in an uncivilized part of the globe. I'm not moving to Borneo."

He looked surprised. "I do not sound that way."

"Yes, you do. You think there is some man standing on a street corner waiting to take advantage of me like I'm a disaster-prone Pauline. This is not the *Perils of Nell.*"

He ran a hand over his close-cropped hair. "How far back did you have to reach for that?"

She laughed. "I lived with an old woman all my life. I even know who Bessie Smith is, and Hattie McDaniel. My grandmother thought culture ended with the death of Billie Holliday."

"I guess there was no Run DMC in your CD collection."

She knew it sounded impossible but it was true. "Only if we could crank it up on the Victrola."

"Your grandmother wasn't that bad."

No she wasn't, but she was happily out of touch. "The only reason I talked Grandma into buying a VCR was that the old movies had started coming out on tape."

They had finally made it to the head of the line, so they scrambled into the taxi and Riley gave the driver their destination.

Nell watched the taxi pull out into traffic, thinking about her grandmother. "I'm going to tell you something I haven't told anyone," she said to Riley.

"You've told me a lot of stuff you haven't told anybody."

"Okay, that's true." She fell silent. Maybe she didn't need to tell him.

"What's your big secret?" he finally asked.

"I'm a lot more like my grandmother than I thought." Now that was hard to say. It was something she could barely admit even to herself. "This is going to sound a little mercenary, but I knew that my grandmother would eventually pass and she would leave me the house and the diner. I've been working at the diner since I was sixteen years old and I put away a minimum of a hundred dollars a month for the last nine years, and with the sale of the house and the diner I figured when my grandmother passed I'd be free to do what I wanted."

A sly smile crossed his full lips. "You've been planning your escape all along."

She nodded. "I was prepared to struggle, but I get to do what I want in a much grander style than I thought."

He reached up and loosened the knot of his red tie. "So that's your big secret?"

Part of her wanted him to tell her she'd been bad, but he seemed more amused. "Aren't you shocked?"

"Shocked, no," he said as he pulled his tie off. "Impressed as hell, yes."

She took a deep breath and laid her hand on her chest. "I needed to get all that off my chest."

"Why?"

"Everyone in Wayloo thinks I'm such an idiot because I didn't know about my grandmother's money, and everyone in town did."

"I knew your grandmother had money. I just didn't know she had that kind of money. Surprise." He unfastened the top button of his shirt. "The apple didn't fall too far from the tree."

The taxi pulled up to the Waldorf-Astoria. Riley paid and helped Nell out.

"How about a nightcap in the bar?" Riley asked.

"Why not?" she replied and tucked her hand around his elbow as they walked through the marble lobby.

As they walked into the bar, two men turned around to stare at her. She'd never garnered so much appreciation before. She knew she looked like she had money, but then a lot of people in New York looked like they had money.

They sat down and Nell noticed a scowl on Riley's face. "What's wrong?"

He inclined his head in the direction of the men. "I don't like the way those guys looked at you."

"Stop being silly. What do you think I'm gonna do, take them both home? I wouldn't know what to do with them. Why are you acting jealous?" Nell said, keeping the men at the bar in the corner of her eye. They had turned back to their drinks and forgotten her.

She turned back to Riley and smiled. She had put him in an odd position; she was asking him to help her lose her virginity, but not become emotionally involved.

"You're thinking again," Riley said.

Their drinks arrived and Nell sipped her wine.

"Implementing my dream has become more complicated than I thought. I expected everything to fall into place like it did in my head, and I forgot about the details because all I was concerned about was the big picture."

"I get what you're saying, Nell. But why me? No holds barred, I want the truth."

"Riley, every woman you've been with since your divorce raves about how magnificent you are in bed. The next thing that comes out of their mouth is your inability to commit to them. I know we've had this conversation before, but I can't have a man in my life who will stand between me and my dreams. You're not capable of loving me and I don't want to love you." Even though I've fallen in love with you anyway. The thought skittered through her mind, shocking her. How had she fallen in love with Riley without knowing and recognizing her feelings? He had made himself at home in her life.

"You said you'd asked me out three times, and, looking back, I have to wonder if you had known I was a virgin, would you have asked me out? Be honest."

He opened his mouth, but nothing came out.

"Let's be realistic," Nell said. "You go out with women to have sex with them."

"Nell, I'm uncomfortable with the direction you're taking."

"Am I wrong?"

He shifted in his chair. "No, but coming out of your mouth, I sound so calculating."

"I know I'm supposed to be a nice girl, get married, have children and do all those by-the-book things, but working in a diner, I've learned a lot about human nature. You got what you wanted without being cold and calculating. And those women understood that all they had of interest to you was their bodies. I want you to treat me like you treated those women and not be so overprotective."

"Nell," he said, taking her hand. "I want this time to be special for you. Losing your virginity is a life-defining moment and I don't want you to come away from the experience with bad memories. I want you to understand the beauty of a man and a woman together."

"Riley…" she started.

He shook a finger at her. "Nell, you listen to this and listen good. I'm letting you out into the big, bad nasty world…"

"I beg your pardon. I'm all grown up."

"Yes, you are, but you are also beautiful and sweet. And as much as you try not to be, you're naive and have a whole lot of money. Do you know what that does for you?"

"What?"

"You have a big target on your forehead and I'm allowed to worry about you. I am your friend."

Nell tilted her head at him, warmed by his protectiveness. *Oh, boy. I have just got myself in a world of trouble. I have to be strong.*

"Come on." He stood and grabbed her hand. "Tonight is the night and we're not delaying this any longer."

Riley stared at Nell in the suite bedroom. The bed had been turned down, the sheets were warm and inviting. Nell stood next to the bed and smiled at him. He had to make sure this was what she wanted. "Are you nervous?"

"No."

He wiped his sweaty hands on his suit pants. "Good. We have to do this right."

She held her hands out. "That's why I came to you."

"Great." *Be cool. You can do this. You've had sex plenty of times in your life.*

"Would you like to undress me?" she asked. "Or should I do it myself?"

"What would you like?" Normally he liked to do the work, but this was her first time so he wanted her to have options.

She turned her back to him. "You undress me."

"Are you sure?"

"Yes."

Riley moved his hands up until the tips of his fingers came into contact with her dress. Immediately he unzipped her dress. The whisper of the zipper filled the room. He leaned over and kissed her spine. She wriggled beneath his touch. Inhaling her clean flowery scent, he knew he was lost.

A thousand thoughts ran through his muddled mind. An inferno raged inside him, consuming him. He fought to keep his hands gentle on her body. Caught between his desire to consummate his growing need for her and his head's demand for caution, he didn't turn her around so he could face her.

Then came the bra. The bra straps slipped down her arms and it hit the floor with a gentle whoosh.

He noticed his hands were trembling. "Are you sure?"

Nell turned around, covering her breasts with her hands. "You asked me that already."

Riley couldn't remember a woman who had

looked at him with such trust and heat. He was honored that she trusted him as much as she wanted him. He felt he'd been given this sacred gift to protect. He wasn't sure if he was worthy. Quickly, he undressed and tossed his clothes over a chair. He stood in front of her feeling as though he was sixteen again and having sex for the first time.

She moved toward him until she was less than an inch away. "Do you have protection?"

"I'm prepared." His voice was hoarse and gravelly.

She smiled and then pushed hard on his shoulder. "Let's go to the undiscovered country then."

"I'm not bringing Captain Kirk, Nell."

"I thought it was from Shakespeare. Just trying to lighten the moment."

"No need." He relaxed and sank onto the mattress. She settled next to him, dropping her hands to reveal her breasts. Her breasts were beautiful, large and round with big nipples. They were the kind of breasts that filled a man's hand. Aching to touch her, he reached up and twirled a strand of hair around his finger. "You are so beautiful. I want you on top."

She bit her bottom lip. "Are you sure? I'm kinda big."

"Nell, we had this talk. Get your lush, sexy, hot body on top."

"Well, okay." She straddled him, planting her hands on his chest. Her breasts swayed. "So are you." She leaned over and kissed him, her breasts brushing against his chest.

Her lips were so sweet and tender, Riley didn't want the kiss to end. He felt her hand slip around his wrist and guide his hand to her stomach.

"Touch me," she whispered against his lips.

The silk underwear was warm and smooth. His fingers slipped under the elastic and between her thighs. Her body quivered at his touch. Riley found her wet and ready for him. He began to stroke her hard bud. Her body undulated as she kept rhythm with his ministrations. He could feel her fingernails dig into his chest.

Perspiration began to glisten on her skin and she matched the pace of his hand. Her body lowered until the tips of her breasts touched his chest. Riley explored her gently, raking her damp curls as he pleasured her. He plunged another finger inside her and she arched her back until they were skin to skin. Slipping his other hand around her to grasp her bottom, he held her so she couldn't move away. But she didn't seem to want him to withdraw. Instead she increased the moving of her body to match his hand's movement.

Riley felt her body stiffen. By the rigid set of her shoulders he knew she approached her climax. He increased his stroking and within seconds Nell tumbled over the edge. She collapsed on top of him and he rolled her on her back. Quickly he stripped off her panties and tossed them aside, then he rolled on top of her.

Nell curled her leg around him, trapping him at

her side. "Oh, my. Thank you. And to think I waited this long."

He stroked her cheek. "Not for lack of trying on my part."

She snuggled up to him. "I want more."

He balanced on his elbow and leaned over to kiss her. "Me, too."

"Well then, let's get to it."

"You are very demanding."

She gave him a throaty laugh. "If I wasn't, we wouldn't be here, would we?"

Riley reached for the condom he'd put on the night table earlier. He could feel Nell's eyes on him. This pleased him. He grasped the red packet and quickly tore it open. Rolling off of her, he sat up. His hands shook as he sheathed himself.

Her eyes sparkled in the muted light. Her face was luminous and her smile inviting. She moved her hands up to cover her bare breasts.

"Don't be shy."

"I'm not being shy." She giggled.

Slowly he moved back to her side. He reached over and stroked her cheek. "Nell."

Nell moved her hands. "I'm all yours."

Riley lowered his head and kissed her. Again, the sweetness of her lips stunned him. She wrapped her arms around his neck.

He wanted to take things slowly, but the look on Nell's face and her half-parted lips nearly drove him to the edge. He planted a trail of kisses up her arm to her neck. Her body quivered under him. Her skin tasted so clean and fresh, he knew he was addicted.

Carefully he kissed a sweet chocolate-colored nipple that hardened beneath the ministrations of his tongue. Nell's breath came out in spurts. Her legs wrapped around his waist, and Riley knew he couldn't take much more. He wanted to be inside her, feeling the spasms of her muscles urging on his own climax.

"Please," she whimpered. "Please…now."

"Easy. Easy. We have time."

"No. I need you now. Make love to me now." Her brown eyes begged him to continue.

How could he deny her? "Anything you want," he murmured against her cheek. He shifted on her body and probed her with the tip of his penis. Nell opened herself wider and Riley eased inside and then pushed until he was totally sheathed inside her. "Damn! Nell!" His body throbbed with want of her.

Nell ran a hand over his hair.

The sensation of her fingers running through his hair sent shivers down his spine. Nell took a deep breath. He squeezed his eyes shut and gave her a gentle thrust. Her body responded.

He opened his eyes and stared deep into hers, seeing the wonder, the surprise and the total acceptance of what he was doing. His jaw tightened. She shifted slightly and he thought he saw a shadow in her eyes. "Are you all right?"

She smiled at him. "I'm perfect." Her voice was low and sultry.

He let her body adjust to him a few more seconds. Her tight wetness nearly drove him insane, but he wanted to make this as good for her as possible. He began to probe her gently, moving deep inside, knowing that no matter how careful he was, she was going to be sore in the morning.

Nell kissed his mouth, his cheek, his chin. She whispered soft words of encouragement.

Each stroke carried him closer to pleasure, each withdrawal gave him a sharper sense of expectation. He pulled back slightly to look at her face. Her skin was flushed and moist.

He was close to release, and didn't think he could hold out much longer. He tried to slow himself down, but her gentle encouragement became more demanding as her body rocked against his. Her muscles tightened around him and he felt her body go taut. Her back arched and she cried out his name. Undulating spasms surrounding him brought him to the brink and with one last thrust, he crashed to his own climax.

Riley lay on his back, one arm around Nell and the other behind his head. The drapes were wide open and bright moonlight lit the bedroom.

Riley loved her. He didn't know when it had happened. Or why it had happened. He just knew he loved her. Nell Evans, the virgin seductress, had stolen his heart. He should have been scared. He should have been mad, but right now he just kinda felt at peace with the world.

She shifted on the bed and moved closer to him. Her lush body curled into his as if she belonged there. Normally he didn't like to touch anybody else during sleep, but Nell's body next to his lined up. The curve of her rear end nestled in his crotch, her back rubbing his stomach. This is what sleeping with a woman was all about.

She sighed and scooted closer. "Riley," she whispered.

He leaned over and kissed her cheek. Inhaling, he could smell the clean, seductive scent of cotton blossom and oranges on her skin. He loved how she smelled. He would never forget her scent, even after she left him for New York.

No. She couldn't leave him. Not now. Not ever. They'd made love. She was his.

The need to possess her forever ran hot in his veins. His heart rate began to accelerate. He broke out in a cold sweat. She couldn't leave him. Because of her he felt alive for the first time since Benjy's death. And she wanted to leave him for some stupid adventure halfway across the country.

"Riley?"

He quelled the raging emotions inside him. "Hey, sleepyhead."

"You were staring at me."

How could he not stare at her? She was perfect in every way possible. "You're beautiful in the moonlight." He ran his finger down the curve of her arm.

"Stop." She cuddled against him, her face shadows and light. "You don't have to flirt with me."

Riley leaned over and kissed her forehead. "Nell, you are worth the full treatment."

Snaking an arm around his neck, she held him close. "I want to make love again."

His body began to react. He was game for another round himself, but he was worried about her. "You have to be sore."

Nell kissed his chin. "A little, but if you're real gentle I think I can handle it."

"How about a nice hot bath?" He bit back a groan as her tongue moved over his skin.

"Can't we do both?"

He thought of the big marble tub a few feet away from them.

His first thought when he'd seen the room was Nell in that tub up to her chin in white fluffy bubbles. Not a bad idea. He shifted away from her and got off the bed. "Give me a sec."

She giggled. "Only a second."

He gave her rear end a gentle swat. "Impatient wench."

She sat up, dragging the sheet with her. "You made me this way."

The words sex puppet jumped into his head, but didn't sit well with him. She stared at him with luminous chocolate-brown eyes. Her long curls had fallen about her head and shoulders. Her lips were lush and bruised. On the crest of one breast he saw a purplish mark—he'd given her a hickey. "No, I didn't make you this way. I just helped you unleash the sex kitten inside."

She fell back on the bed laughing. "I am such a naughty sex kitten." She threw her arms up. "Thank you. Thank you. Thank you."

The low sultry sound worked its magic all the way into his soul. He clenched his fists at his side, and walked into the bathroom. Seeing the woman inside unleashed, so free and so wild, left him speechless. He'd never known a woman to take such innocent pleasure in sex before. Not even Chloe.

He began to shake. His sweet little Nell was going to fly away from him now and he would never get her back.

"I don't hear any water running," she yelled from the bedroom.

Riley walked over to the bathtub and turned on the hot water. He flipped the stopper and watched the water fill the tub.

What the hell had he done?

Nell faced Riley in the big bathtub. She felt absolutely decadent. Steamy water and fragrant bubbles surrounded them. A faint scent of vanilla rose from the warm water.

She didn't know what it was, but something was wrong with him. Had she been a disappointment in bed? Her first time and she knew she hadn't done everything right, but she'd be better next time. "Riley, what's wrong? Was I that bad?"

He smiled and reached up and put a dollop of bubbles on her nose and she sneezed.

"No, baby, you were wonderful. You were everything I always knew you would be."

Nell wiped the bubbles off her nose. "Are you sure?"

Riley leaned over and grabbed her around the waist, pulling her toward him. "Everything is perfect."

"Good. I thought maybe you were a bit disappointed in me because I didn't know what I was doing."

He kissed her. "You were born for this. I'm glad you shared it with me."

His kiss lingered on her lips and she felt a thrill vibrate through her. "Make love to me again."

His eyebrows rose. "In the bathtub?"

"I saw it in the movies once. I'd like to try it."

He grinned wickedly. "I want you on top."

"Why?"

"So I can look at you when you come."

Her mouth fell open. Warmth slid up her cheeks. He'd used very earthy words before during her initiation, and even though she found his language exciting, she couldn't seem to control her embarrassment.

"Was that too dirty for you?"

"No, but…"

He put his fingers on her mouth, silencing her.

"Slide over me. I think you'll like being in control."
Quickly, he put on the condom.

Nell moved over his legs and his hips. Riley
placed his hand on the small of her back to steady
her. Slowly she lowered herself over his sex, easing
him inside. She was a little sore, but she would never
admit it. She didn't want him trying to protect her
now. She had too much time to make up for.

She bit her bottom lip to keep from crying out.
She felt herself stretch to accommodate his hard
length. Her internal muscles contracted and gripped
him, holding him deep inside her. She didn't want
this moment to end. This perfect moment of anticipation, of pleasure, she wanted to hold it forever. She
loved him. There was no doubt, she was madly, ir-
revocably in love with Riley Martin. A hard breath
escaped her mouth.

"Look at me, Nell."

She couldn't open her eyes. If she looked at him,
he'd know she loved him. She couldn't let that
happen or this would be over.

Chapter 14

Nell walked into the diner and stopped to stare. The place was packed for breakfast with a line of people sitting on benches outside waiting to get in. Nell had never known the diner to have so many people so early in the morning. Even Sheriff Atkins sat at his place at the snack bar wolfing down a huge stack of pancakes.

And the place had changed. New drapes hung from the windows and the walls were now a rich reddish-brown. She'd only been gone a few days, not two months.

Lucy placed a plate of fruit in front of a customer, then looked up and smiled. "You're back. How was your trip?"

"I settled everything." Nell approached her mother. "What did you do to the diner? It's so different."

Lucy waved her hand. "I just added a few touches. I closed the place down for a day and gave it a thorough cleaning and then repainted. I hope you like it."

Nell wasn't sure how she felt about it. The place looked so different. "But…the walls are so…red."

Lucy grinned. "I was reading this article in a magazine that said red stimulates the appetite, so I'm stimulating some appetites."

Even the pink uniforms were gone. Her mother wore a white blouse and a pencil-slim black skirt. Nell noticed Dee Dee wearing the same uniform. "And you got new uniforms."

Lucy ran a hand down her hip. "Don't you like it? I thought they make us appear more upscale."

"I do." Even Dee Dee looked good instead of like a bubblegum-pink prostitute. Her blouse was buttoned all the way to her neck and she wore a little black bow tie beneath the points of the collar.

Nell recognized most of the customers, but she didn't recognize two of the waitresses. "And you hired some new people."

"I had to. With all the changes this place is really hopping." Lucy grinned.

A young man came out from the kitchen, plates balanced on his arm. "That's Bobby Atkins."

"He's going to the community college, but was accepted at Duke for the spring semester so I arranged with his daddy so he could make a little extra money." Lucy smiled encouragingly at Bobby. "He took to waiting tables like that." She snapped her fingers. "All his customers just love him."

"I'm sure Sheriff Atkins had to twist your arm," Nell said drily.

Lucy held up her left hand to show a gleaming white ring with a diamond the size of a basketball. "You have to help family, sugar."

Oh, my God. Her mother had gone and got herself engaged. Nell didn't know what to say. "I go away for a few days and you change the diner into some upscale bistro. And get yourself engaged." What was going to happen when she left for good?

Her mother's eyes sparkled with pride. "Business is up three hundred percent and people are coming in from Thomasville and Sparks and Stanley. I am so excited. I think I finally found my calling."

"And a husband!"

Lucy giggled and shot a loving look at Sheriff Atkins. "I feel twenty years old again, and without all the drugs and the booze…" Her mother hesitated. "I'll tell you that story sometime, but not now. Come see the carpet samples I picked out. It's going to be installed next week."

"Okay." Nell didn't remember giving her mother permission to make all these changes, but if things were this good after a few days, she wasn't going to complain.

Lucy dragged Nell to the back office and flung

open the door. A pile of catalogs were on the desk, a book of carpet samples leaned against the wall. The computer hummed in the center of the desk and Nell saw an Internet site advertising tablecloths, china and glassware for restaurants.

"I know you're gonna sell the diner and I want you to give me the first crack at it. Leonard is thinking about retiring and he wants to help me run the diner. I have some money set aside. Not much, but I think it's enough for a down payment. But we can get a loan for the difference. At least I didn't kill my credit in all these years."

Nell's head whirled. "I don't know what to say."

Lucy patted Nell's arm. "You think about it and let me know. And if you decide not to, you'll get a ton more money because it's been redecorated and business is really good. You sit here and look through the catalogs. I'm thinking of new chairs and tables. Something more upscale than chrome and Formica."

"But, Mom—" Nell said, but her mother was gone, flitting out the door and across the dining area waving at people and stopping at a few tables to talk.

Nell sat down at the desk and stared at the catalogs. What had happened to her mother? How could she *not* sell the diner to her after making all these changes?

Grandma was wrong. Lucy had been redeemed.

Lucy came back into the office and closed the door. Nell watched her mother with trepidation. Lucy pulled up a side chair and sat across from Nell. "Everything is going well out there, but I got to thinking you need to know some things about me and the past."

Okay, Nell thought. Things were going well. Did she want to listen to this?

Lucy took a deep breath. "It's come time for me to make amends and since things went so well in New York I'm figuring you're leaving soon. So I need you to sit there and listen before you say anything."

Lucy stroked her skirt with shaky hands. "First of all, I'm so sorry I wasn't the mother you needed me to be."

Nell wasn't sure if she wanted to deal with this at the moment, and opened her mouth to stop her mother's confession.

Lucy held up her hand. "No, let me talk. If I don't get it out now, you'll never understand." She took another deep breath. "When I was young, after my daddy left, Mama put me on her version of lockdown. I hated every minute of my life. The only thing I could think to do was rebel. I did everything I could think of to shame her and make her angry and make her stop loving me. And I did that. The second I had a chance to leave, I did and I never looked back. That is until I got myself pregnant with you. No way was I gonna let a baby interfere with my good times. So I had you, dropped you off with your grandma and left again. And I did a lot of things I'm ashamed of and probably the biggest one was the drugs. I know that's not an excuse for my behavior, but the best thing I ever did was give you to your grandmother, because there would have been no telling how you would have turned out with me for a momma."

Nell could only stare at her mother. She didn't know if she was ready for this kind of honesty, but obviously her mother was. Her best course of action was to shut up and hold on to everything she was feeling right now. Even though she was sad and a little resentful, she did understand, and in a way she respected the fact her mother had made the best decision for Nell, because living with Grandma had worked out.

"About five years ago," Lucy continued, "I was on my last nickel. Your grandma had been sending me money and it was going faster than anything. I woke up one day in bed with this strange man and I started to wonder just what the hell I was doing. I got up, put on my clothes and went to this place called Tranquility House and checked myself in. And for a long time I worked on kicking the drugs."

"So you went to rehab?"

Lucy nodded sadly. "Next to giving you up, checking myself in was the hardest thing I'd ever done. And taking a hard look at my life was even harder. I got myself together and it took a long time. I know I can never be your mother. My mama did a good job with you and you turned out to be something so much more than I could have asked for. You are sweet, you're beautiful, intelligent and kind. I don't deserve you." Tears filled Lucy's eyes. "I hope one day we can be friends."

"How long have you been clean and sober?" Nell asked.

Lucy pulled a key chain out of her pocket and held up a charm of the number five. "Five years, Nell."

Her mother had one of those awards from Narcotics Anonymous. "That was you then, wasn't it?" Nell said.

"What?"

"Just before I left for New York, I saw an announcement in the newspaper for someone putting together an NA chapter. And that was you."

"That was me. I am serious about working my program and finding some middle ground between you and me, even though you're leaving."

"I'm overwhelmed," was the only thing Nell could say.

Lucy smiled. "In a good way, or a bad way?"

She wasn't sure. "Since we're having this honesty between us, you need to know. For a long, long time, I tried every day not to hate you. I thought I'd done something bad and that was why you left me for my grandmother to raise."

"Not you. Me. I didn't have the right stuff to be your mama. And I wasn't going to drag you all over on my tail like a piece of luggage. I did what I thought was right and seeing and knowing you now,

I made the right decision. I am so proud of you, Nell. And so is my mama."

Nell leaned forward and kissed Lucy on the cheek. "I need time to think, but I'm proud of you, too."

Lucy wiped the tears away and stood up. She straightened her black skirt, opened the door and sashayed out with her head held high. Nell watched her mother cross the dining area. Lucy laughed and joked with a customer and then walked around the snack bar and opened the pie chest. Sheriff Atkins leaned over the counter and gave her a little kiss on the cheek and she nodded, her gaze darting back toward Nell.

Nell smiled and stood up, closed the door, and went to sit back down at the desk to think.

Riley's house smelled wonderfully of something cooking. Nell sniffed, trying to identify what it was, but the tantalizing aromas weren't giving up their secrets.

She walked to the back door and looked through the window. Riley stood in the middle of the kitchen with a cookbook in his hands. He looked up at the stove and frowned, then walked over to it and picked up a long wooden spoon.

Nell knocked, he looked at her, smiled and beckoned her to come in. "What are you cooking?"

"I'm not sure. I can't pronounce the words."

She laughed and took the cookbook from him. Having been raised on relatively plain fare, one glance told her even she couldn't pronounce the French words either. At least she knew they were French. "I don't like to think of myself as country, but right now I'm country." She handed the book back. "At least it smells delicious."

"I have high hopes. I'll know when the beef is done, but I'm not quite sure if my other flavors have mingled. Maybe we should call Chloe. She's all big on this kind of cuisine."

"Are you kidding?" Nell said as she tipped back the lid to a pot and sniffed. "She would insist on coming over, fixing the food and then cleaning up. Let's have an adventure and cook the meal ourselves."

"Okay, peel the carrots." He pointed at the sink where a bundle of carrots rested with their green stems wilting into limpness.

She picked up the peeler and started in. The kitchen fell silent except for the occasional rattle of a pan lid as Riley stirred something. "Riley, do you realize the recipe you're cooking is for eight people?"

He flicked on the oven light and Nell saw a huge roast inside, sizzling away. "I thought the roast was a little big, but I'm a man and I like leftovers."

Nell only laughed. "And that's a good thing, because you are gonna have leftovers."

"So how do you feel about your trip to New York?"

"I'm beginning to feel settled. Even things around here are getting settled."

"Such as?" he asked as he frowned over the open book.

"I had an interesting chat with my mother today."

His eyebrow rose. "That statement sounds a little ominous."

"I was surprised, to say the least." She found peeling the carrots soothing, but as the pile grew, she wondered how many Riley really needed. She sneaked a look at the open book, and counted again. She could stop peeling. She even had extra. "My mother isn't the devil incarnate I used to think she was."

"Is that a good thing?"

Well, it meant she had to change her view of her mother, but she could handle that. "She seems to have settled down in her life. She and Sheriff Atkins are getting married, she wants to buy the diner and she wants to be friends."

"Hmm."

"That's all you have to say?"

He adjusted the flame on the stovetop. "A wise man never interferes between a woman and her mother. Besides, you have that lethal peeler in your hands and I think I'd better stay neutral until I know which way the river is flowing."

Well, aren't you a bucketful of help? "But you're my friend."

He took a sip of his beer and placed the bottle on the countertop. "When Chloe and Daphne started throwing down, I got the heck out of town."

Nell laughed. She knew exactly what Riley meant. Daphne had been fodder for the gossip mill for years. She was a wonderful person, but she did things her way.

"How do you feel about your mother?"

"I'm okay about her buying the diner. I don't know how I feel about her marrying Sheriff Atkins. He's a good man, and he appears to love her passionately, but I don't know how I like the idea of him being my stepfather. Especially when I have no idea who my real father is. I'm twenty-five years old and suddenly I have a mother and a father." The sensation was odd beyond words.

"Maybe she doesn't want to be your mother, and I know Sheriff Atkins has enough going on with his own kids."

Nell swiped the carrot shavings into the sink and into the garbage disposal. "Lucy did say she wanted to be my friend, and that pretty much threw me for a loop."

"Then be her friend. You're not going to be living here and seeing her every day."

"True." Nell reached over and flipped the switch and listened to the grinding for a few seconds. She liked Riley's kitchen. He had all the modern conveniences. She flipped off the disposal. "I guess I need to let go of the past as I'm heading into my future."

Riley rattled a few more lids and glanced into the oven at the cooking roast. "Do you ever think about your father?"

Nell's hand clenched. "When I was a kid I used to dream he'd come and rescue me. But then again,

I wasn't unhappy. Now I have the money to find him if I want, but I don't know if Lucy knows who my father is and I don't think we're at a point in our relationship where I could ask her."

"Why not?"

Because it would seem like Nell was slapping away her mother's efforts to make peace. "She's working hard to put her past behind her. She told me she's been clean and sober for five years. I have to let her have her chance, too." Until this moment, Nell hadn't seen the parallel between herself and her mother. Lucy wanted to have her chance. She'd wasted a lot of years, just like Nell. "For a long time, when I was younger, I ended up on the wrong side of every bully this town ever had. I lived in a little fantasy world so I wouldn't have to deal with the hurt."

"Nell, I swear to God, you are one of the most kindhearted women I know."

She smiled at him. Did that sound like a bad thing? "Being hateful and nasty takes too much time and effort and what do you have in the end? A lot of people who hate you at a time in your life when you are gonna need them." Lucy had caused a lot of pain for her mama, and Nell had to remember that Lucy was trying to make amends. If Lucy was big enough to admit her mistakes, Nell had to be big enough to accept her mother's overtures and let the past go as well.

Riley poured her a glass of chilled white wine and she sat at the kitchen table and watched him prepare the carrots. Part of her wanted to tell Riley he needed to let the past go, too. He was hanging on to so much of his pain and grief he couldn't see the future. She saw all his faults clearly and loved him for them anyway. She would never admit to him how she felt. He would always have a place in her heart.

"You're looking at me," he said.

"Just thinking."

He sat down opposite her and took a sip of his beer. "About what?"

She took a deep breath and tilted her head. There were so many things that she couldn't grab on to just one. "Of many things."

"Not to distract you from thinking, but I've been thinking, too. I want to make an offer on the Collier farm."

She remembered their peaceful afternoon on the porch swing. "I'm not surprised."

"I want to pay fair market value." He took another sip of beer.

"If I were an astute businesswoman, I would try and take you for every penny I could get."

"You would? After I just complimented you on your kind heart?"

Nell laughed. "I know. I just have to give you a hard time." She thought a moment. She'd just looked at the appraisal for the farm and knew what her grandmother had paid. She rapidly calculated what she knew about land values in Wayloo at the moment. "I'll sell you the farm. Market value is at

$500,000 and I'll sell it to you for $450,000. We'll start the paperwork first thing in the morning."

Riley looked stunned. "Just like that. No dickering! No negotiating! No trying to squeeze every penny you can out of me."

"Nope." She smiled, enjoying his confusion. And the fact that she was able to make him happy. "You're not buying that place to develop it, but because you want it for yourself. The Collier farm is a good place to live. It's peaceful, beautiful and it's a good place to start building memories."

"How do you know I'm not going to divide the property and put houses on it?"

"You're not," she said confidently. "You're going to restore that old house to its former glory and you're gonna make it home."

"Thank you, Nell."

"What are friends for?"

He grinned at her. "Are you going to divest yourself of everything in Wayloo?"

"Pretty much. I don't know what Lucy's plans are, but I'll keep the house for her to live in until she decides. I decided to keep one foot in Wayloo." Not even she could completely sever her roots. "And now that Lucy and I are going to work on our relationship, I'll need to come back." Her grandmother had invested in a lot of property around Wayloo and Nell was torn between selling it all and keeping it for the rental income. If she kept it, her ties to Wayloo would never be severed, but if she sold it, she could look for investment property in New York which would appreciate at a much faster rate than that in Wayloo. She needed to grow her money.

Decisions. Decisions. She sighed. She was trading a whole way of life for a dream. At times she felt like she stood on the edge of a precipice. She'd waited for so long to start living her life and her tics to Wayloo still held her back.

Riley stood and went to the stove. Nell set the table and then sat down again as Riley served dinner.

She forked the roast into her mouth. "This is mouthwatering delicious, Riley."

"Thanks, Nell."

He didn't look happy. "Something on your mind? Care to share with me?"

"No, nothing we need to talk about."

Nell fell silent, wondering what he was avoiding. He'd just given her the typical I'll-be-fine man thing. She didn't want to press him, but after they finished eating and she helped him clean up the kitchen, she couldn't help wondering just what was really on his mind.

Riley was absolutely beautiful. He stood in front of her, sliding his shirt off his shoulders. His chest flexed and the muscles beneath rippled. He reached out to her and she grinned as he unsnapped the top button of her jeans and she knew she was in trouble.

He freed the other snaps and pulled the flaps open. He leaned forward and kissed her on the stomach. She sucked in a quick breath. Then he ran his tongue along the elastic of her panties. She bit her bottom lip, not wanting to cry out.

He pulled her jeans down her legs and then off, tossing them behind him. He cupped her bottom, and a shiver ran up her spine as he sat her down on the bed.

She leaned back on her hands, giving him full view of her in nothing but white thong panties and her shirt. Heat spiraled through her and she watched him watching her, impatient for him to continue.

His eyes moved up and down her. Then he grabbed the ends of her shirt and raised it over her head. Her hair fell about her face and she shook her head to get it out of her eyes. She didn't want to miss a moment of Riley's seduction of her.

He reached for the waistband of her panties and she eased her hips up as he slid the thong off. She pointed to his pants. "Take your pants off, too."

"Yes, ma'am."

The bulge in his jeans started her heart racing. This was getting better and better.

He stood, pushed his jeans down to his ankles and pulled them clear. Underneath he wore black silk boxers.

"Riley," Nell said, "you are so beautiful."

"I'm glad you approve."

She reached to unfasten her bra, but he stopped her hands and put them down to her side. She gave herself over to his touch.

He skimmed his hands across her belly. Under his touch her stomach contracted. Instead of unhooking her bra, he slipped a tapered finger under the lacy cups. Her nipples peaked the second his fingers came in contact with them.

He began to massage her breasts slowly. The back of her bra began to bind her skin. He unfastened the front hook and her breasts sprang free. He hooked the straps with his fingers, and pushed them down and then tossed the bra over his other shoulder.

Riley sucked in a breath. "You're perfect." He cupped her breasts in his hands, then lowered his head to suckle each large nipple. A shot of desire struck through her that went straight from her breasts to that secret area between her legs.

Nell lowered her eyes, unable to stand the raging desire she saw reflected back at her. "Thank you."

"Only stating the obvious." Tracing the sides of her breasts, he used his thumbs to knead the hardened nipples.

His erection grew. The rush of sexual heat bloomed in her and she couldn't stop herself from trembling. She wanted him so bad she hurt. Nell leaned her head back and gave herself over to the sensation.

Riley lay back and pulled her on top of him. "You feel so good." He massaged her hips and rear end, running his hands lightly over her skin.

Nell slipped her legs on each side of his waist and sat up. She slid her hands across his broad chest, delighting in the play of sinew contracting under her touch. "You have no idea how turned on I am at this moment."

He smiled. As his lips curved into a wicked grin, he grazed his finger along her hip across the curve of her stomach and down between her legs. "Let's find out."

Nell stiffened and lifted herself off Riley's stomach as his finger glided inside her. She could feel the moist heat of her desire spill from her.

Her internal muscles contracted as soon as his finger came into contact with her sensitive bud. Nell thought she was going to die. His index finger teased her, tormented her, excited her as he made tiny circles inside her. She concentrated on his actions.

"You are so sweet." His laugh was husky and low.

Peeking out from beneath her lashes, she saw desire darken his eyes almost to black, and she wriggled her hips to increase his access to her. She wanted to say something, but what? He had already exceeded her wildest fantasies.

Riley pressed her closer with a hand on her rear end. "Nell, open your eyes."

She did as he commanded, knowing she didn't want to miss a single moment. Focusing on his mouth, she thought no man had a right to lips so beautiful. Full and sensual, his mouth looked wicked. She loved his mouth. And she wanted him to put his mouth everywhere on her.

Riley slipped his other finger into her and quick-

ened the pace of his massage. He opened her up
with one hand while pressing on her from behind
with the other. His touch was incredibly arousing
and tender. The naked pleasure in his eyes gave her
as much gratification as his erotic kneading.

Her breasts bobbed with every motion of her body.
Bending over, she attacked Riley's mouth, plunging
her tongue inside. She caressed his tongue with her
own.

Nell squirmed under his intense stroking. Friction
and pressure increased and she gave herself over to
her passion. Her nipples grazed his sweat-slick chest
and the heat nearly burned her. Her stomach tightened.

Riley's fingers played inside her, rousing her
higher and higher, until her body began to float.
Grinding her hips against his hands, Nell took
control of the lovemaking. She feasted on his mouth.
An ancient rhythm drove her. She wanted release. A
groan exploded in her throat. She hadn't thought
she was capable of such noise or such pleasure.

"That's it. Let go," he whispered against her lips.

"Riley."

"Come for me."

Her body began to pulsate. The pressure inside
her built until she couldn't stand it anymore and her
muscles spasmed. She threw her head back and let
out a long low groan that built in intensity with the
pulsing muscles inside her. Tears gathered at the
corners of her eyes. *Grandmama,* she thought, *you
were so wrong about sex.*

For a brief second her body seemed to hang over a chasm. Then everything shattered and her world erupted around her, inside her, over her. Heat engulfed her and she began to tremble and rock. The uproar lasted forever.

Nell tried to catch her breath, unable to stop her body from shaking. Opening her eyes, she stared directly into Riley's. She wanted to say something but words seemed so inadequate.

"Feeling better?" Riley asked, grinning.

She nodded her head, unable to speak.

"I'm glad you liked it. I enjoyed watching you."

She reached over and tugged on the waistband of his boxers. "What about you?"

"Honey, we have all day."

"I want you inside me." Nell reached over and touched his cheek. "Make love to me."

"What was I just doing?" The bulge was so evident in his boxers that she wondered how he could walk. "Let me get a condom."

Riley reached over to the nightstand and opened the drawer. Noticing that his hand shook as he reached inside, she realized he was as affected by her as she was by him. She heard Riley's bare feet slap against the hardwood floor as he neared her.

Riley walked around to the foot of the bed with a wicked grin on his face. He stopped in front of her, and his gaze zeroed in on her mound.

"Very pretty."

Nell closed her legs and sat up, laughing. She

grabbed the waistband of his boxers and eased them down. The black silk pooled at his feet. She bit her bottom lip. "Talk about pretty."

He raised the condom packet to his mouth and bit down on one corner, then ripped off the top.

She sat up and held out her hand, waving her fingers. "Can I put it on you?"

Riley shook his head. "I'll be done before we start if you do."

Disappointment engulfed her, but she understood. He slipped the condom on.

He was so beautiful standing there ready just for her. She felt thankful she'd chosen him to show her the art of making love.

"I'm waiting." She scooted farther up the bed to lean against the pillows.

Taking a deep breath, he got on the bed and crawled over to her. She smiled at the glitter of passion in his eyes. He brushed hair off her cheek and she caught his finger and lifted it to her mouth. "Make love to me," she said, as she licked his finger and then daintily nipped it.

He snaked an arm around her waist and fell back, pulling her on top of him. "I want to watch you."

"You want me on top?"

"More than anything."

She took a deep breath. "Well, I think I can give that a try." She moved over and straddled him. Positioning herself over him, she bit her bottom lip. This wasn't quite like their bathtub encounter at the Waldorf-Astoria, but something even better.

He sucked in his breath as she slid herself down over his erection. The second she touched the tip of his penis, she felt warm wetness spread through, lubricating her. When he was just inside her, he gripped her waist and stopped her from sliding all the way down. "Riley, what's wrong?"

He grinned at her. "I want to make this last."

"We have plenty of time." She understood exactly how he felt. She wanted the same thing. He pulled her down, sliding into her, and her internal muscles contracted around him.

Riley ran his hands up her body, and she gloried in the feel of his skin. His spicy scent curled around her. Nell kissed his chin, his cheeks, and nuzzled deep into the crook of his neck.

She sat up, and he cupped her breasts. They fitted so perfectly in the palms of his hands. She was made for him.

She ground her hips and watched his face contort, knowing he was close to the edge. Her body was on fire.

She pumped up and down, melting their bodies into one. Slowly the ecstasy built. Her muscles clenched again and she cried out as her body spasmed, shattering into a thousand shards of glass. For a moment she thought she would die.

In the back of her mind she knew something had changed. She didn't know what, but she would never be the same. She hung suspended in time and space, her body vibrating with the shuddering climax that seemed to go on and on. When she finally came back to earth, Riley kissed her deeply.

"I love you," he said.

Riley lay in bed waiting for her to respond to what he'd said.

"You can't love me." Her voice sounded desperate.

He sat up. "Why the hell not?" After all, he'd loved her for years.

"Because I'm not staying in Wayloo and it's stupid for you to love me."

"But you don't have to leave. Pretty much everything you want to do in New York you can experience here." He touched her and she jerked away to sit on the edge of the mattress. Not quite everything, he thought.

In the darkness of the room, she was a dark silhouette against the moonlit window. The slope of her breasts, the curve of her waist and the tilt of her head left him wanting more. More than he ever wanted to give up again.

"Yes, I do have to leave, Riley." Her voice sounded hoarse with sorrow. "I can't give up my dream now. I've never wanted anything else, never stopped dreaming about getting out of here. That's why you can't be in love with me."

Tell her, he thought. *If you don't tell her now,*

she'll never know. "I've loved you since high school. Hell, since I was a kid." He knelt behind her and curled his arms around her shoulders. Her skin was hot and moist and he could feel her breath on his skin.

"How can you love anyone? You can't even get over Benjy's death."

He stiffened, not expecting her to say that. "That's a low blow."

"But true." She shrugged him away and stood up, reaching for the big robe he'd loaned her. "Benjy was everything to you and you haven't been able to pick up the pieces and move on. That is why I chose you. I knew you couldn't give me real love. You have never worked out your grief for your son."

Of course he'd dealt with his grief. He put it away in a box in the very back of his mind, and that was dealing with it. "I've moved on." He sounded defensive even to himself.

"No, you haven't. You can't even buy a head-stone, or visit Benjy. That's not moving on, that's standing still."

He jumped to his feet and glared at her. "Don't judge me."

"I don't have to. You keep judging yourself."

Riley stood stock-still. "What the hell makes you so smart?"

She put one hand on her hip. "I just spent the last twenty-five years standing still."

"You don't know anything." His voice caught.

He remembered Benjy's first day in preschool and the way he'd loved being with the other kids. He remembered the broken body on the street and the way Benjy's eyes had looked at him and then gone dazed and unfocused as the light went out of him.

Nell put a hand on his arm. "Do you think you're the only one who suffered? What about Chloe?"

"I tried, but I couldn't do anything for her." He felt a sob in his throat.

"You couldn't because you were too wrapped up in yourself to see Chloe's grief."

"Who the hell do you think you are?" he yelled as he pushed her away and jumped off the bed, even though he knew what she was saying was true.

"You think I don't know what I'm talking about. Try living for a quarter century with a woman whose husband and daughter left her, breaking her heart so she has nothing left to give you. You know why my grandmother left me all her money? Because she had nothing else to give me. She didn't have anything so she didn't even try, but deep down inside, my grandmother was broken. You're broken, too. You think you love me, but you love your grief more."

He couldn't take the pitying look in her eyes. He turned away to stand by the window and leaned his head against the cool glass. He heard a rustle and when he turned around, Nell was gone.

Nell sat at her desk in the back office of the diner. She fingered the ownership papers of the diner. This had to be the right move. She had to get away from Riley. If she didn't she'd never leave him or Wayloo ever. Every dream she'd ever had of moving to New York City and becoming her own person would die. She needed to reinvent herself. Away from Wayloo, she had no past. No expectations. Except for the one she decided to make for herself. She would love Riley forever. She knew he would never leave Wayloo, she wouldn't even ask him.

A knock interrupted her thoughts. Lucy. "Yes?"

Nell patted the ownership papers. "Give me a dollar."

"A dollar?" Lucy looked confused.

"One buck."

Lucy pulled money out of her pocket. "I can spare ten."

Nell held up her hand. "No, just one dollar."

Lucy turned over the dollar and Nell pushed the paper toward her. "You just bought yourself a diner."

Lucy stared at the papers. "Nell, are you sure you want to do this?"

"Yes," Nell said in a determined voice. She didn't want to think about the diner, or Riley, or the hurt that wouldn't go away.

"The diner is worth a lot more than a dollar," Lucy said with a frown. "I'm more than willing to pay a fair price for it."

"No," Nell said, holding up one hand. "Not another word." She pushed the papers toward Lucy. "Look everything over. I made an appointment with

Billy Ray to make the transfer. He's expecting you at three." Nell stood up and looked around the office, remembering her grandmother sitting at the same desk making out the payroll or ordering supplies. "You now own this place."

"I don't know what to say, Nell." Lucy looked as if she was going to cry.

Nell hugged her mother. "The diner belongs to you now. The time has come for me to let go." She walked out of the office with her head held high. She wouldn't give in to her tears. She marched through the dining area, determined not to cry in front of the customers.

She pushed open the door and walked right past Chloe with only a slight nod. She couldn't say good-bye. Not yet. Maybe tomorrow.

Nell stood in the center of the living room trying to decide what to take with her. A clock her grand-mother had gotten at an antique shop in New Orleans ticked merrily away. She would take that. She'd always loved that clock and though her grandmother hadn't been one for extravagance, something about the little clock had drawn her it to it, too.

She didn't want much, because when she deco-rated her apartment she'd pick furniture she liked. New life, new clothes, new furniture. That's how her life should be. She would leave bright and early the next morning. She had one more thing to do. Riley.

She heard the front door slam and footsteps sounded in the hallway.

"When the hell were you going to tell me you were leaving tomorrow?" Riley demanded as he walked into the living room.

Nell remembered the first time he'd touched her. Lucy had interrupted. "I was going to call you tonight."

He looked sad and defeated. "Don't go, Nell."

She touched his arm. "I thought we settled this." The pain in his eyes wrenched at her. She picked up a large manila envelope. "I'm glad you stopped by. Here's the paperwork for the Collier farm. Billy Ray tells me you've talked to the bank already and the loan will be funded in a week or so. Go see him and he'll make sure everything is done right."

He looked like a lost little boy and her heart went out to him. "Nell."

"I explained everything to you more than once now." She tried to keep an even tone to her voice. She didn't want him to know how badly she felt. "I want a new life. I can't have that here."

"I love you," he said.

Her heart was breaking, too. "I told you, you can't love me. We agreed right in the beginning, no mushy love junk." And he'd reneged and she'd hardened her heart to him. No matter how she felt, her future wasn't with Riley.

He looked at her, disappointed. "Fine, then. Go have a new life. Have a great time in the Big Bad Apple."

"Don't hate me, Riley. Please."

He didn't say anything. He just turned around and walked out.

Nell stood in the center of the living room, listening tensely to the slam of his car door and the sound of the motor as he started it up. She slumped onto the couch.

This was for the best.

For both of them.

Right?

Epilogue

Three Months Later

Riley consulted the list in his notebook. He'd almost gutted the Collier house, getting rid of the dry rot he'd discovered in the wall studs and on the second-floor landing. He'd traced the root of the problem to an old leak in the roof and fixed that, too. Though the inside was far from finished, it was liveable if he chose to move in. He had just a few more things to do, and then what?

He looked around, thinking of how he would paint the room. A house as gracious-looking as this would require a careful decorating hand. For that he would need someone else. He could fix and restore houses, but putting the final touches needed an expertise he didn't have.

A car sounded on the drive, gravel crunching beneath the wheels. He glanced out the picture window in the living room and saw Chloe get out of her car. He'd asked her to come and he was glad she hadn't refused.

She turned around and from the smile on her lips, he could tell she approved of what he'd done so far.

She stepped around a wheelbarrow and a pile of wood to make her way to the front door.

"Come on in," Riley said as she poked her head in to see where he was.

She glanced around the living room, approval still on her face. "You've done a nice job. Nell would approve."

Riley felt a glow of pleasure at her words. And he sincerely hoped Nell would like the house. Restoring the old farmhouse had been the only thing that kept him sane whenever he thought about her. "I was just thinking about you."

Her eyebrows rose curiously. "Why?" She ran a finger over the fireplace mantel.

Riley had found it in the barn under a pile of hay. From what he could tell, the wood was hand-carved and it had probably been the original mantel. "I'm going to need some decorating advice."

"If I decorate it I'm going to have to buy it, and I don't have this kind of money."

Riley laughed. "I'm not selling."

"You're not living either."

"What the hell do you mean by that?"

She crossed her arms over her chest. "For the last three months, I could count the number of times I've seen you in town. You've really been engrossed in fixing this place up. Which leads me to ask myself, what is the purpose of a single man wanting a six-bedroom house?"

He gestured widely. "It could be an investment for me."

"Riley," she said, "this is Chloe you're talking to."

Okay, did he tell her what he wanted or was he afraid she'd think he was crazy? "I have plans for this house."

"What kind of plans?"

The gleam in her eyes unnerved him. "I'm not telling." He hadn't even admitted to himself yet what he wanted to do.

"I stopped by to visit Benjy this morning."

Riley tensed, wondering if she would be okay with his choice. "And?"

"I like the headstone you purchased."

Choosing the headstone had been one of the hardest things he'd ever done. For the first time, he realized that the reason he'd delayed was because of the finality the headstone represented. "You don't mind I didn't ask you?"

"No," she replied with a small smile. "You needed to pick that headstone more than I did. I especially like the little angel on a motorcycle. Benjy loved that bike of yours."

The motorcycle was parked in the barn right now. Riley had been thinking about something for a long time and now he wanted to start a dream of his own. "He did, didn't he?"

"Why now?" Chloe asked.

Because he had accepted his life as it was, not the way he wanted it. "I have to move on. You were right. Nell was right. Hell, I think all of Wayloo was right. By leaving that headstone undone, living with my guilt, I thought I wouldn't forget him. But I realize now he'll always be in my heart."

"Riley, I wish our marriage had worked out better. You have always been a stand-up guy. I loved your compassion."

"But it wasn't enough to keep us together."

She sighed. "We were both going through our own hell, and we didn't know how to be there for each other."

"Can you forgive me?" he asked in a humble tone.

She stared at him, tears dripping down her cheeks. "There's nothing to forgive, Riley."

He folded her into his embrace. "Thank you." He wiped the tears from her eyes.

"I stayed your friend because you needed me. But since we are friends, I'm going to be brutally honest with you. You need to go to New York and bring Nell home."

He patted his pocket. "I have my ticket. My house is almost completed. That was my plan all along."

"Why did you wait three months?"

Nell had needed this time, and he loved her enough to give it to her. But the house was ready and his bed was lonely. "Because Nell needed her taste of freedom. I figured three months was enough time for her to figure out if she's liking New York or not. If she likes New York, we'll figure out a way to make it all work there, but if she doesn't and she's just rolling along on pride right now, I can bring her home with her pride intact."

"Back that up," Chloe said. "How do you plan to work around New York City?"

He dug into his pocket and pulled out a business card. "You remember Burke Ivy."

"You went to college with him."

"I called, and I have a job with him in New York anytime I want."

Chloe's eyebrows rose almost to her hairline. "You're going to give up Wayloo for New York City?"

Hell, yeah, like that was much of a choice. "If Nell has a yen for Sri Lanka, I'd go there."

"You've done a lot of growing these last couple of months, Riley."

"You said I had to. For a long time, I was content to kick back, let you do my laundry and do my shopping. I wasn't moving. Life moves and a person has to move with it or it will mow you over. I want Nell."

"You've always wanted Nell." She smiled,

looking him up and down. "And now you've finally become the man she needs."

Nell could do this. This was her moment of truth. After all, wasn't this what she'd dreamed of? What she wanted all her life? To be the quintessential New York City woman. She'd left behind everything she'd ever known. She'd left behind love and Riley. Darn it, she was going into that bar. Remote was the "it" bar in Manhattan.

Swallowing her trepidation, she walked to the front door. The doorman pointed to her. She was in. A thrill crept up her spine. He unhooked the velvet rope and she stepped through. Loud music assaulted her. A crush of people swallowed her up as she made her way to the bar. Several handsome men smiled and made eye contact with her. Their predatory smiles made her nervous.

"Hello, pretty stranger."

Nell looked up into smiling green eyes. The handsome man seemed familiar. His dreadlocks hung nearly to his waist. His bulging muscles looked as if they were fighting to get out of his tight black T-shirt. "Hi."

He bent down. "I'm Sam."

She immediately recognized him. Sam Dylan, the actor on the soap, *Forever Tomorrow*. Oh, my God. She held out her hand. "I'm Nell."

Sam slipped a hand around her elbow. "Nice to

meet you, Nell. Let me take you to one of the private rooms."

"Of course." Imagine Nell Evans, small-town nobody, being escorted to a private room by Sam Dylan, aka soap stud. No one in Wayloo would ever believe chubby old Nell, the wallflower, had one of the hottest men in the world wanting to spend a little time with her.

She should be thrilled. This was supposed to be her dream come true, but something was missing. She knew what it was. She missed Riley. She still wanted Riley. New York City wasn't enough. But she'd burned that bridge. She'd have to make do with her new life.

They entered a small room with a black leather sofa and a glass-topped table. Paintings of lithe nudes covered the wall. The music filtering through the speakers was romantic guitars, not the techno band playing outside.

"Have a seat," he said. "What can I get you to drink?"

"Cola."

His sparkling eyes went wide. "And?"

Okay, she was showing her small-town roots. Three months and a person would think she'd get it right, but she'd discovered alcohol just wasn't for her. "A vodka martini."

He picked up the phone and ordered. Then he sat next to her. "Where did you get that accent?"

"Do I sound like a hick?"

"No." He scooted closer. "Like Scarlett O'Hara."

"I'm from Mississippi."

"A Southern belle." His smile widened. "I love Southern girls."

At least he wasn't making fun of her, like some of the people she ran into in this city. She was fine until she opened her mouth. "Not anymore. I'm a New Yorker now."

He propped an elbow on the back of the sofa. "I hope not."

"Why?"

"The second I saw you I knew there was something different about you and I liked that something different."

Well, he was sweet. Not like most of the men she'd already met who wanted to go from "Hello," to "How do you like your breakfast eggs—sunny-side up or over easy?"

"Oh."

"What's your story, Nell from Mississippi?"

Nell opened her mouth to give him some pithy I'm-trying-to-find-myself remark, but realized after about five sentences into her answer she was telling him about what a fool she'd been for dumping Riley and how she really didn't like New York and if she went home people would think she was a failure. And she couldn't get Riley back because she had been mean to him.

She didn't remember starting to cry, but when she put her hand to her face, she found her cheeks wet with tears. "I really thought this is the life I wanted, but I hate it here." And she wanted to go home, but she'd said terrible things to Riley and knew he didn't want her back.

"I know how you feel."

How could a man as cosmopolitan as Sam Dylan feel like he was out of his depth? "You do? How?"

"I'm from Baker, California, home of the world's giant thermometer. And I got fired today."

She reached out and touched his hand. "I'm so sorry."

He glanced down at their hands. "You are just the icing on the cake of my bad day."

"How?"

"I was hoping for a temporary playmate, now I feel like I'm consoling my little sister. Kinda kills the action, if you know what I mean."

She bit her lip. "I'm sorry."

"Don't be." Sam put his hand on top of hers. "You need to go."

"You're right. I should go home and go to bed."

He shook his head, his locks swirling around him like thick black snakes. "I don't mean that. You need to go back to Wayloo and back to Riley."

What the hell was he talking about? "I can't."

"Trust me as a man. All you have to do is show up."

"You think so?"

He gave her a long, critical look and then nodded, as though something extremely important had just occurred to him. "We're going back to your place to pack some clothes, and I'm taking you back to Wayloo." He stood and tossed a crisp hundred on the table. "I have nothing else going on in my life. By the way, where the hell is Wayloo?"

Riley filled the auto feeder for Chester. He stuffed enough food into the feeder for at least a week. Chester could get out into his dog run through the pet door in the garage.

Though Riley intended to be back in two days, with or without Nell, he didn't want Chester to starve if he wasn't successful on his first attempt at talking to her.

She'd had her three months. He'd let her find herself, but now was the time to come home.

"Wish me luck, boy," Riley said as he grabbed his jacket and slung his duffel bag over one shoulder.

Chester barked and sat down, tail wagging as though he'd understood every word.

Riley locked the back door, checked the stove and made sure the security timer was set. As he walked down the hall to the front door, he heard a knock at the door. Probably Chloe to give him another death threat if he didn't come back with Nell. He went to the door and opened it. Some guy he didn't know was standing in the entranceway.

"You Riley?" The tall, familiar-looking brother with the long dreads filled up his entire doorway.

"Yes."

"This is for Nell."

Pain exploded in his head. Everything went black.

* * *

Riley was dreaming. He lay on the floor and Nell sat next to him talking in a soothing tone and sponging off his face with a cold cloth. Riley could even swear he smelled cotton blossom and orange. Only one woman smelled like that. He didn't know he could smell in a dream.

"Riley?"

Now he was hearing her voice. He was going to kill the guy who hit him. But the dream of Nell was nice. Usually he dreamed of her naked and in his bed with her legs wrapped around him and her breasts tight against his chest. But this dream was nice, too. He didn't want to wake up.

"Riley, sweetie, wake up."

Now his dream was talking to him. "If I wake up you won't be here."

"Wake up, Riley."

He forced his eyelids to stay shut, so he could keep on dreaming. "I'm not waking up. Not yet," he murmured.

The soft touch of fingers moved slowly across his cheek. "I'm here now."

He forced his left eye open, because his right one wouldn't budge. Nell's face swam into view. A shaft of morning sun slid between the strands of her dark hair.

"Nell! You're here!"

"I'm home, Riley. Home for good."

Nell had come home. How? He couldn't remember how she'd gotten there. "Did I come back from New York and not remember?"

She laughed. "No, I came back to Wayloo."

"I swear I was going to get you and make you come home." He tried to lift his head. "Until that train hit me."

Her hand was on his shoulder, holding him down. "That wasn't a train, that was Sam Dylan."

Why was Nell with someone named Sam Dylan? The name seemed familiar and then he remembered Chloe's favorite daytime drama, as she called it. Someone had to explain this to him. "Do you mean, Sam Dylan, the actor?" Where had Nell met an actor? Jealousy flooded through him. She'd come back to tell him she was gonna marry the guy.

"Yes, Sam drove me home."

"From New York City?"

She nodded. "Every mile of it. In his Escalade. I really want an Escalade."

"Why did he hit me?"

Nell shrugged. "I think it was, in Chloe's words, 'a man thing.' He was being protective." She ran her hand slowly over his face. If his head would stop ringing, he might even enjoy her touching him. "I won't let him hurt you again."

He pushed himself up on his elbows. He had to get his manhood back. "I'm ready for him now."

She patted his shoulder. "Chloe already showed him what she learned in her kickboxing class. You're going to have to be nice. He's a little lost right now and he's going to stay in Wayloo for a while at Chloe's Bed-and-Breakfast."

"Just tell him to stay out of my way."

"I will."

"Why didn't you fly?"

She sat down on the floor next to him and crossed her legs. "Well, it was a spur-of-the-moment kind of thing."

"Why did you come back?"

"My dreams didn't work out like I thought they would."

He forced himself not to smile. She was back. "Am I your backup plan?"

"You were always my dream." Nell ran a finger over his bottom lip. "I just didn't know it until a couple of nights ago."

"Do you know it now?" He sat up. His face was about an inch away from hers. He couldn't quite keep his emotions packed down. He didn't want to hope, not quite yet.

"Yeah, I do." She palmed his cheek. "We drove by the cemetery. I saw Benjy's headstone. It was perfect."

"It was time."

Her bottom lip quivered. "How are you doing?"

How was he doing? He'd laid his past to rest, he was ready to embrace his future—now that he knew the future would include Nell. "I'm better. I'm at peace. There was nothing I could do to save him. I had him for four years. I was lucky. That's better than most people."

She smiled. "I'm glad."

"I want to make babies with you, Nell. I want to make a life with you. I want to love you until I die, but only if you've gotten over trying to be something you're not. You belong in Wayloo. You belong with me."

"I know." She laced her fingers through his. "You were the best adventure I ever had. I had to go halfway across the country to figure that out. I want to spend the rest of my life having adventures with you."

"I fixed the Collier house up. I did it for you. I did it for us."

"How about that rickety old porch swing?"

He jiggled his eyebrows. "I fixed the porch swing."

She put her arms around his neck. "I'm going to love you forever, Riley Martin."

"Good." He bent his head. Inches from her lips, he said, "I'm going to hold you to that, Nell Evans." He pulled her lips to his. He wasn't going to let this woman out of his sight. Not now. Not ever.

From boardroom to bedroom…

Brenda JACKSON

In Bed with Her Boss

Though D'marcus Armstrong is a demanding, cranky
boss, he's the star of Opal Lockhart's fantasies. But
what chance does a buttoned-up, naive secretary have
with this self-made millionaire? A pretty good one
actually…when Opal's sisters come to the rescue
with a makeover and some attitude adjustment!

THE LOCKHARTS
THREE WEDDINGS & A REUNION

*Available the first week of August
wherever books are sold.*

KIMANI™
ROMANCE

Was she worth the risk?

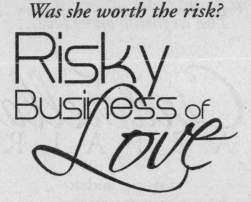

Risky
Business of
Love

Favorite author

YAHRAH ST. JOHN

When the powerful attraction between reporter
Ciara Miller and charismatic senatorial candidate
Jonathan Butler leads to an affair, they are forced
to choose between ambition and love. Jonathan
knows the risks but feels Ciara is worth it…until
dirty politics shakes up his world.

*Available the first week of August
wherever books are sold.*

The negotiation of love…

A Cinderella AFFAIR

Favorite author
A.C. ARTHUR

Camille Davis is sophisticated, ambitious, talented…and riddled with self-doubt—except when it comes to selling her father's home. No deal, no way. But Las Vegas real estate mogul Adam Donovan and his negotiating skills are leaving Camille weak in the knees…and maybe, just maybe, willing to compromise?

Available the first week of August wherever books are sold.

KIMANI™
ROMANCE

www.kimanipress.com   KPACA0310807

Sometimes life needs a rewind button...

USA TODAY BESTSELLING AUTHOR

KAYLA Perrin

Love, Lies & Videotape

On the verge of realizing her lifelong dream of becoming an actress, Jasmine St. Clair is suddenly embroiled in a sex-tape scandal, tarnishing her good girl image. Desperate to escape the false accusations, Jasmine heads to the Caribbean and meets Darien Lamont—a sexy, mysterious American running from demons of his own.

"A fine storytelling talent."
—*The Toronto Star*

*Available the first week of August
wherever books are sold.*

ARABESQUE®

www.kimanipress.com   KPKP0160807

Essence bestselling author

PATRICIA HALEY

Still Waters

A poignant and memorable story about a once-loving
husband who has lost his way…and his spiritual wife
who has grown weary from constantly praying for
the marriage. Greg and Laurie Wright are perched at
the edge of an all-out crisis—and only a miracle can
restore what's been lost.

"Patricia Haley has written a unique work of
Christian fiction that should not be missed."
—*Rawsistaz Reviewers* on *No Regrets*

*Available the first week of August
wherever books are sold.*

Adversity can strengthen your faith....

TIME FOR *Hope*

MAXINE BILLINGS

**A poignant new novel about the nature
of faith and of friendship...and the ways
in which each can save us.**

Two years ago, Hope Mason was cruelly betrayed by
her husband and best friend. Now, with no desire or
energy to socialize, Hope believes the fewer friends
one has, the better. But when she's asked to train
young Tyla Jefferson, Tyla shows Hope how to open
up again—and helps Hope discover that life is not
nearly as hopeless as she thinks.

*Available the first week of August
wherever books are sold.*

Celebrating life every step of the way.

YOU ONLY GET *Better*

New York Times bestselling author

CONNIE BRISCOE

and

Essence bestselling authors

LOLITA FILES
ANITA BUNKLEY

Three fortysomething women discover that life, men and everything else get better with age in this entertaining three-in-one anthology from three award-winning authors!

Available the first week of March wherever books are sold.

KIMANI PRESS™
www.kimanipress.com

KPYOGB0590307